Spirit

the Castle Rock Cougar

Dan Bomkamp

Lovstad Publishing
Poynette, Wisconsin
Lovstadpublishing@live.com

ISBN: 0692490620
ISBN-13: 978-0692490624
Previous ISBN: 0615752071

Printed in the United States of America

Cover design by Lovstad Publishing
Cover photo by Dan Bomkamp

DEDICATION

This book is dedicated to my biggest fan, Mom.

Acknowledgements

Thanks to my publisher and friend, Joel Lovstad, for his help with this and all of my books. Over the years we've collaborated on a lot of stories and ideas and I always am glad for his input.

Cover Photo

Thanks to Brandon Maloney for helping with the photo.

Other Books by Dan Bomkamp

The Adventures of Thunderfoot
More Adventures of Thunderfoot
Thanks, Thunderfoot
The Gosey
Big Edna
Voyageur
Lost Flight
Whiteout
Tag

Spirit

Chapter 1

The dog jerked her head up and stared into the darkness. She turned her head sideways, ears up, alert. It was pitch black inside the tent but she had heard, or maybe sensed something outside. She sniffed the air and the hair on the back of her neck stood up stiff. Her body became rigid and deep in her chest she began to growl. The growl grew louder and louder and she got halfway up on her feet.

"Sally, what's wrong girl?" her master whispered. The dog growled louder and began to rise. "Sally, what's wrong? Come on, it's OK, you're OK," Aidan Grant said to the dog.

"She acts like she hears something outside," whispered his best buddy Dylan Mahoney from the other side of the tent.

"Yeah, I know but what would set her off like this? There's

nothing around here that she's afraid of."

The dog stood up and started barking loudly. She moved toward the door of the tent and then came back to her master frantically wanting to get outside.

"Dylan, make sure the tent's zipped up tight," Aidan said. "Maybe it's a skunk and I don't want her getting out and ending up covered in skunk spray."

Dylan crawled out of his sleeping bag and checked the zipper. Sally followed him to the door. "It's tight," he said. "Come on Sal, its ok there's nothing out there that's gonna hurt you."

Suddenly they heard a slight clunk from outside. The dog began to bark furiously. "Sounds like something bumped into our cooler," Aidan whispered.

Dylan said, "Should I go out and check?"

"Go ahead if you're brave enough," Aidan answered.

"Well, actually I'm not that brave," Dylan said with a chuckle.

Sally stopped barking and stood very still listening. Then she came back to the space between the two boys and lay down. Her ears were still up listening but she seemed to be much calmer.

Aidan put his arm around the dog. She was shaking.

"Whatever it was, I think it's gone," Dylan said.

"Yeah, it seems like it," Aidan said. He flipped open his phone and looked at the time. "It's only a little after 4am let's sleep for a while yet."

"Yeah, good idea," Dylan said.

Aidan put his arm around the dog and she snuggled up to him and in no time they were all sleeping again.

Aidan and Dylan were frequent visitors to this place they called The Big Valley. They were best friends and had grown up on adjoining farms in the northern part of Grant County Wisconsin.

This part of Wisconsin is in the un-glaciated part of the state known as the Driftless Area. It is known for its deep valleys and steep wooded hills. The Big Valley is at the northern most part of Aidan's family farm and is a secluded place that has only one way in and out. The valley is surrounded by steep hills and at the northern border it is protected by steep rock cliffs and towering pines that makes the area look almost prehistoric. A small creek runs out of a large spring in the rocks and meanders down the floor of the valley for the entire length. The stream gets larger near the lower end of the two mile long run and leaves the valley through the only entrance to the place which is a narrow gap in the hills that has a trail that is just wide enough for a 4 wheeler or snowmobile.

Trout and suckers are abundant in the stream and many years prior, a family of beaver built a dam across it and that resulted in a pond about an acre in size. It was a great place to fish and hunt and the two boys had grown up spending much of their spare time there.

On this day they'd come home after a baseball game at the school and gathered up their tent and a few groceries and gone to the valley to camp out and then fish and scout for spring turkey hunting which was coming up in a short time.

Aidan woke and could feel the heat coming off the nylon tent as the sun beat down on them. Sally was staring at him, her tail wagging. He smiled at the dog.

"Hey Sal, are you feeling better this morning?"

The dog wagged her tail faster and began slapping it against Dylan.

"Jeez Sal, you're beating me," Dylan said turning over. He grabbed the dog and hugger her. "You gotta go out and go potty?"

The dog jumped up and ran to the door. Dylan crawled over and zipped open the tent and she ran outside. He crawled out the door in his underwear right behind her. Aidan could hear him walking a little way away and then heard the distinct sound of something splashing on the ground.

"Cripes you could have gone a little farther away," he said through the tent. "You're fouling our campsite."

11

"Oh baloney, don't be such an old woman," Dylan said.

Aidan sat up and scratched his head and crawled out of his sleeping bag.

"Holy crap!" Dylan said.

"What?"

"The cooler's gone."

"What? Are you sure?"

"Of course I'm sure. It was sitting right next to the 4 wheeler and now there's nothing here."

Aidan crawled out also in his underwear and walked over to the vehicle. "What the... Who would come all the way back here and steal a cooler with a little food and a couple of sodas in it?"

Sally was sniffing around the vehicle and her hair stood up on her back as she sniffed. She followed the scent on the ground toward the hillside but when she got up to the edge of the woods she stopped and stood staring into the brush. She stood there for a minute and then turned and walked back to the campsite.

"She must have smelled whoever took the cooler."

"Yeah, but who would take it? And if someone came all the way back here and took it why would they go up into the woods instead of going back down the middle of the valley?"

The two boys stood there looking into the woods trying to figure out the mystery.

They both seemed to get the same feeling at about the same time. Aidan turned and said quietly to Dylan, "Do you get the feeling we're being watched?"

Dylan nodded. "Spooky isn't it?"

They stood looking intently at the woods trying to get a glimpse of someone moving but saw nothing.

"Let's get dressed and get out of here," Dylan said. "Our breakfast was in that cooler and I'm starved."

Aidan laughed. "You're always starved, but I agree, let's go

12

back and get something to eat and then we can come back and do some fishing and turkey looking."

Dylan crawled into the tent and retrieved their clothes and shoes and they dressed and zipped the tent shut. Dylan got onto the 4 wheeler and Aidan sat on the back on a luggage rack they'd attached to it so they could take Sally with them on their trips to the valley. Sally hopped up next to Aidan and they turned and drove along the stream to the gap in the hills.

Aidan kept watching up on the hill for a sign of their intruder but saw nothing.

Up on the hill a pair of eyes watched them move down the valley.

Chapter 2

As they pulled into the farmyard at Dylan's family farm his father came out of the barn. They drove the vehicle over by him and stopped. Sally jumped off and ran up to Dylan's dad and he gave her a good ear scratching.

"She's sure a big loving girl," he said stroking the dog's golden fur. "I think all golden retrievers are like that, big lovable goofs."

"That's for sure," Dylan said, "but last night she got pretty excited when someone snuck into our camp and stole our cooler."

"Stole your cooler! Which cooler are you talking about?"

"That little one, the red and white one... it's just big enough for a few sandwiches and some pops. We had some eggs and bacon in it for breakfast but someone took it while we were sleeping in the tent."

His dad looked incredulous. "Why would someone go all the way back there to steal a $10 cooler and some bacon?"

The boys shrugged. "It had to be somebody just messing with us. I don't think there are any animals that could carry a cooler like that. A raccoon couldn't and I doubt a coyote would be able to either. It had to be somebody just screwing with us."

Aidan looked at Dylan. "You don't suppose it was Clifford and that stupid Sonny do you?" he asked.

"Those dopes are stupid enough to do it but I don't think

14

they have enough ambition to walk all the way back there. If they rode back on a 4 wheeler or their dirt bikes we'd have heard them wouldn't we?"

"Clifford who?" his dad asked.

"Clifford Stewart and his pet dummy Sonny Summers," Dylan said. "They have a little bit of a grudge about Aidan and me and the baseball team. It seems that they thought they were the best pitcher and catcher duo on the team and then Aidan and I took over that starting job and they thought it was an unfair decision on the coach's part. They've been pushing us for a few weeks about it but so far we've just been laughing at them. Maybe it's time to have a heart-to-heart talk with them."

His dad grinned. "I wouldn't suggest fighting... unless it was necessary, but I'm sure you two can hold your own against almost anybody in your school. Maybe you should let them know you won't take any harassment."

The boys nodded and grinned. "We've got practice this afternoon, I think we might mention it to them," Dylan said. "Right now I'm starved and I think there's some bacon and eggs in the kitchen with my name on them."

"Where's the Brute?" Aidan asked.

"I think he's in the house," Dylan's dad said. "He's not a morning person and he thinks the barn is for cows and not dogs."

They all laughed and headed up to the house. When Dylan opened the door his dog Brutus, an English Bulldog looked up from his bed next to the fireplace and woofed. "Hey Brute, are you hungry?" he asked.

The dog got up and waddled across the room and began play fighting with Sally.

"Good God, I hope those two never mate," Aidan said.

Dylan laughed. "What are you saying.......my dog is ugly?"

"He looks like a sumo wrestler, with Jabba the Hut's head," Aidan said.

"Brutus, kill Aidan!" Dylan said pointing at Aidan's throat.

The dog just looked up and slurped his tongue across Aidan's hand.

"Well, close enough," Dylan said.

They washed up and Dylan began making them some breakfast. His dad had eaten earlier and his mom was in town so he filled a pan with bacon and Aidan put some bread into the toaster. When the bacon was crisp Dylan cracked a half a dozen eggs into the pan and soon they were sitting at the kitchen table eating.

Aidan looked up at the wall to a picture of the two of them at about age 12. They were standing in front of the pond in the valley in cut off shorts and shirtless with their arms around each other's shoulders, while each held up a stringer with several trout on it. They had big cheesy grins on their faces as only best friends can when posing for a picture.

At that time they were both about the same size but in the past 4 years Dylan had stretched up and now was about 6 feet 2 and built like a linebacker. His hair had darkened to a medium brown which he kept cut in a medium length. He had deep brown eyes that always looked like he was hiding a little secret that gave them a twinkle. Aidan had stopped growing taller a few inches short of 6 feet but had also bulked up to an athlete's build. His hair had stayed lighter and he also wore it in a medium length. The light hair went well with his blue eyes.

"We've grown up a little since then," Dylan said when he saw his friend looking at the picture.

"Yeah, we sure have. It's amazing isn't it, we've been friends since we were babies and I don't think we've ever really had an argument or fight."

"That time you shot me in the butt with your paintball gun at almost point blank range was about as close as we've come to a real argument," Dylan said.

Aidan laughed. "Yeah but I knew you were really pissed so I let you shoot me in the butt to make up for it. Damn my butt cheek was black and blue for a month!"

They ate in silence for a bit and then Aidan said, "Do you think it was Clifford?"

Dylan shook his head. "No, I don't. First he wouldn't walk all the way back there, second it was 4 in the morning and third why would he steal just the cooler? There were fishing poles, tackle boxes, other camping gear all over the place, why would he just take the cooler?"

"That's what I was thinking too. When we go to practice today let's kind of bring it up and see what he says, but not push it."

'Yeah I think that's a good idea. We've got another bigger cooler we can take back tonight. That is, if you're not scared to camp again tonight."

Aidan laughed. "I'm not afraid... not one bit. Tonight I'm taking my single shot 12 gauge along just in case our cooler thief returns."

Chapter 3

Later that morning Dylan borrowed his dad's car and they drove to the athletic field for baseball practice. They usually didn't practice on Saturday but it was near the end of the season and they had a chance for the playoffs so the coach asked them to put in the extra effort.

"Are you going to try for your license next week?" Dylan asked.

Aidan nodded. "I'm turning sixteen on Wednesday and have an appointment for my road test on Friday."

Dylan grinned. "Think you'll pass?"

"I better or I'll never hear the end of it from you," he said.

They arrived at the field and put on their cleats and began playing catch. Most of the team was there except for Clifford and Sonny who drove up shortly after they began warming up. Aidan watched the two of them to see if they seemed like they were acting strangely but didn't see anything that was unusual. Clifford and Sonny began playing catch a little way away from them and after a few minutes Sonny threw a wild throw and it nearly hit Dylan in the back of the head.

"Watch out where you're throwing that thing," Dylan said as he picked up the ball and tossed it back.

"Oh don't worry... if it had hit you in the head it wouldn't have hurt anything," Sonny quipped. He and Clifford began to laugh and giggle at their joke.

Dylan just shook his head and he and Aidan walked to the dugout. "I'm going to talk to those dopes and you sneak over and check out their car and see if they'd be stupid enough to have the cooler in it someplace," Aidan said.

Dylan nodded.

Soon Clifford and Sonny strolled into the dugout and Aidan said something to them about the team they were playing next. As they talked Dylan slipped over to the parking lot and checked the car out. There was nothing inside that he could see, so he reached in and flipped the lever that opened the trunk. He slipped back to the back of the car and looked inside. There was a cooler there but it wasn't theirs. There was also a bunch of beer bottles and other junk. Dylan reached up to close the trunk when Clifford appeared around the side of the car.

"What the hell are you doing in my trunk?" he asked.

"I'm looking for my cooler."

"Why would your cooler be in my trunk?"

"Because somebody stole it last night while we were camping and your name came up first on our list of suspects who'd do something like that. Is that good enough reason?"

"I oughta tell the coach you broke into my car and have him call the cops," Clifford said.

"Go ahead, and while we're at it he can ask you about why your trunk is full of empty beer bottles."

Clifford stopped and stared at Dylan. "Someday, just you wait." He slammed the trunk shut and stomped off to the field.

Dylan trotted back to the infield and shook his head when Aidan looked his way.

On the way home after practice Dylan said, "It wasn't there but that doesn't mean they didn't take it."

"I think we're all wrong about them doing it," Aidan said. "I still think it was some animal. Otherwise why not take more stuff or more valuable stuff. The cooler probably smelled like food since we used it to make sandwiches and cut up stuff on the lid. I think it was an animal."

"But what kind of animal would it be?" Dylan asked.
Aidan shrugged.

They got another cooler and put some food and pop into it, stopped at Aidan's for some other goodies and then headed back to the valley for some late afternoon fishing, supper and a campout.

When they got to their campsite everything was in order. The tent was zipped up tight with their sleeping gear, the metal grate was sitting on the four rocks that held it above the fire and their pots and pans were in their plastic tote sitting right where they'd left them. "Well, nothing is missing," Aidan said.

Sally sniffed the ground and worked her way around camp as the boys got their fishing poles ready and began fishing. They sat on a couple of old lawn chairs that they'd left there some time ago, took off their shoes and cast out into the pond. In no time they began to catch suckers, and now and then a trout. They released the suckers and put the trout on a metal clip stringer.

"They're biting today," Aidan said reeling in a particularly nice brown trout.

Dylan nodded. "I think we should have fresh trout for supper."

It didn't take long and they had six nice fish on the stringer.

"That's plenty for supper," Aidan said.

Dylan agreed, "I think I can eat a couple, how about you?"

Aidan nodded. "You clean up four of them and I'll cut up some potatoes and get them frying. Leave the other two on the stringer and we'll take them home for your grandma."

They went about their chores and some time later they were enjoying fresh trout and fried potatoes. Sally was sitting in between them getting bites from both of them and got filled up nicely too. The sun was just dropping over the west side of the hills when they cleaned up the pans and dishes. Dylan stowed the cooking gear away in the tote and they settled back in their lawn chairs.

"You know, we're pretty darn lucky to have a place like this," he said.

Aidan nodded. "Yeah, like our own private little paradise. We can fish, hunt, trap, and camp back here and not a soul will bother us. This is a real special place. It's like being back 10,000 years ago."

Dylan yawned. "I think I'm ready for sleep," he said.

They got up and opened the tent. Dylan crawled in first and stopped when he got his feet at the door, wiped the dirt off the bottoms and then went all the way in. Aidan did the same and soon they slipped off their tee shirts and pants and crawled into their sleeping bags in their boxers. Sally waited until they were situated and then snuggled in between them. She wiggled a little and then let out a long sigh.

"I guess Sal is ready for bed," Aidan said grinning at the dog.

"Me too," Dylan said.

Aidan reached up and snapped off the battery operated lantern. "Good night," he said.

"Night," Dylan replied.

Aidan had no idea what time it was but it was very dark. Sally woke him as she had the night before with a deep growl.

"Sal, what's wrong?" he whispered.

He put his hand on the dog's back and her fir was standing straight up. "She hears something," Dylan whispered.

Soon the dog got to her feet and growled louder. "You think we should go out?" Aidan asked.

"You forgot the gun didn't you?"

"Dang, yeah, I did. I'm not going to shoot anybody anyway. I thought it might scare them but like I said I don't think it's a person."

"I'll go if you will," Dylan said.

They crawled out of their sleeping bags and Sally began to bark and jump at the side of the tent. Suddenly they heard their utensil tote rattle.

"Someone's out there!" Aidan said. "Keep Sal in here, I'll take a look."

Dylan put his arms around Sally's neck and held her. Aidan zipped the tent flap open and peeked out. Just then he heard the sound of water splashing and their metal stringer jingling.

"Someone's messing with our fish."

He crawled out of the door and turned toward the pond. It was very dark and what little light there was came from the stars. The rattle came from the stringer again but it was up behind him nearer the woods. He turned and looked but all he could see was a large shape as it disappeared into the brush at the hillside. He stood there looking into the night and then felt a shiver go up his spine. He turned to see if anything was behind him but it was clear.

"It wasn't a person," he said as he crawled into the tent and zipped it shut.

"What was it, a coon or something?"

Aidan shook his head. "I don't know what it was but it was bigger than Sally."

 Chapter 4

"What do you mean bigger than Sally? Was it a dog?"

"It was shaped like a dog, low down like that, but it moved real smoothly, more like a cat."

"It'd be a heck of a barn cat to be bigger than Sally," Dylan said. "Are you sure it wasn't somebody crawling into the brush?"

'Dyl, I don't know for sure. I just got a glimpse of it and it was dark enough that I really didn't see much. All I know it that it moved real quickly and was low to the ground."

They settled down into their sleeping bags again and got Sally calmed down. A short while later they were all sleeping again.

Aidan woke to the sound of Dylan passing gas and began to chuckle. "Jeez, what a pig," he said.

Dylan began to laugh. "That's a morning kiss for you."

"Yeah thanks, but your breath smells just like it did yesterday."

"Ouch!"

He began to pet Sally. "Well old girl, what do you say we go over and see if you can trail that intruder after we have breakfast?"

Sally's tail thumped. She had no idea what he was saying but she was glad that he was talking to her.

They got up and dressed and took turns washing up and brushing their teeth in a wash pan filled with water from a kettle they'd heated up on the fire. Aidan opened the cooler and put some sausage links into a pan and Dylan took a jar filled with pre-made pancake batter out and began making pancakes in another pan. In no time they each had a stack of pancakes and sausages. They poured some syrup over the plates and sat back in their lawn chairs looking out over the pond. A wood duck was paddling around on the other side and a muskrat was working in the reeds.

"Dang, I wonder what the poor people are doing this morning," Dylan said grinning at his best buddy.

"I bet whatever it is, it's not as cool as this," Aidan said.

"So you think Sal can track that whatever-it-is?"

"I don't know. She can find a wounded duck in the middle of a marsh. I'd think she could smell an animal on dry land. We'll see."

They shared with Sally and when they were done they cleaned up their mess and put things away.

"Come on Sal....let's go see if we can find that critter that took our fish."

They walked across the valley floor and up to the edge of the woods. "I think it was right about here where I saw it last night," Aidan said.

Sally began sniffing around and suddenly her hair went up on her back and she started moving up the hill following a track. The boys moved along behind her trying to keep out of her way as she worked back and forth on the scent.

"She smells it," Aidan said.

They worked their way up the hill and toward the cliffs at the end of the valley. They were half way up to the top when Dylan said, "Look there's something orange and white. It looks like our cooler." He was pointing up the hill a little way to a mound of dirt sticking out of the hillside.

They climbed up and sure enough their cooler was lying on the mound and it was all torn up. The lid had been chewed off and the cooler was smashed and broken....and empty. "Holy smokes, something destroyed it getting it open," Dylan said.

Aidan picked up the lid. "Look at these gashes. Whatever tore it open had some pretty big teeth."

"Jeez, you think it was a bear or a wolf?"

24

"I don't know, I really have no idea," Aidan said.

Sally meanwhile had moved further up toward the cliffs and stopped to look up into the rocks. The boys came up behind her and she seemed to be very tense. "She knows something's up there," Dylan whispered.

Aidan nodded. They moved up a little farther and Sally stopped to sniff something in the grass. "Hey, she found our stringer," Aidan said.

He reached down and picked up what was left of the metal stringer. The clips had been torn free, no doubt when whatever took it tore the fish off it. There was no sign of the fish but there was something that caught the boy's eye.

"Look at that!" Aidan said.

"Holy smokes," Dylan replied kneeling down in the soft dirt. "That's a cat track Aidan."

Aidan nodded. "That's a heck of a big cat track."

Dylan put his hand flat on the ground next to the track and it was just slightly larger than the imprint of the animal. "Do you think it's a bobcat or a lynx?"

"I'm not sure Dyl, but I don't think they're that big. They're like the size of a beagle or smaller, this is a big critter."

"You sure it's not a bear track?"

"No way, it's a cat for sure."

They stood there and looked up into the rocks. "There are caves up there, a perfect place for a cat like this," Aidan said.

"A perfect place for a cat like what?" Dylan said, even though he knew what the answer would be.

"It's a cougar Dylan, a mountain lion."

"It can't be, there aren't cougars in Wisconsin."

"How do you know for sure? Just because they're not suppose to be in this part of the world doesn't mean one hasn't moved in here."

"But... no way."

"Dylan do you remember three or four years ago, one of our first deer hunting years when that kid shot that bull elk? It was really snowy and foggy and this kid who was about our age shot a spike bull elk."

"Yeah, I remember that now that you mention it. I remember the DNR at first took it away from him and threatened to fine him, but people got real upset so they changed their mind."

"Remember what they said about the elk? There are no elk in Wisconsin, haven't been any for a hundred years."

Dylan laughed. "Yeah, they looked pretty foolish when they said that, and then in the paper the next week there was a picture of the kid and a not-elk."

"I know cougars aren't suppose to be in Wisconsin, but I'm willing to bet this critter is a cougar."

"What are we going to do about it?" Dylan asked.

"For right now we're not going to do anything. Let's keep it to ourselves. We need to get on the internet and do some research into cougars and their territory. I don't want to say anything until we know what's real and not real."

"Good idea." Dylan said.

They both looked up into the jumble of rocks and the sheer cliff faces. If there was a cougar living in the valley, this was its home.

"Come on, let's go," Aidan said slapping his thigh to get Sally to follow him. The dog came along quietly but kept looking over her shoulder into the rocks.

"Sal's nervous," Dylan said.

"So am I."

 **Chapter 5**

"Wait a minute," Aidan said. "I'm going to run down to the campsite and get my phone and we'll take a picture of that track."

"Ok, I'll keep Sal with me. I don't think she should be snooping around up on those rocks if that cat is up there."

Dylan sat down on a log and called Sally over and told her to lie down. Meanwhile Aidan loped down the hill and across the valley to the tent, grabbed his phone and started back up the hillside.

"Whew," he huffed, "It's sure a lot easier going down than back up here, this hill is steep!"

"Why do you think I didn't argue about staying behind," Dylan said grinning.

They walked over to the ground where the cat track was and Dylan knelt down and put his right hand next to the print. Aidan took a picture and then had Dylan move his hand to the other side just to be sure they had one good picture. "Ok, got it," he said.

They hiked down the hill and secured their campsite. They washed the pans and dishes, put them into the tote, snapped the lid down tight and put it inside the tent. Then they put their sleeping bags into plastic bags to keep the dampness off them and zipped the tent up tight.

They got onto the 4 wheeler and headed home.

"*Puma concolor*" Aidan said. "Also known as a cougar, puma, mountain lion, mountain cat, catamount or panther depending on the region, is a mammal of the family Felidae, native to the Americas."

He and Dylan were in the computer lab at school the

following Monday during their study hall.

"This large solitary cat has the greatest range of any large wild terrestrial mammal in the Western Hemisphere, extending from Yukon in Canada to the southern Andes of South America. Holy smokes that's a long way," Dylan continued.

"Yeah, I had no idea they were found all that way," Aidan said. He continued reading, "An adaptable generalist species, the cougar is found in every major American habitat type. It is the second heaviest cat in the American continent after the jaguar. A capable stalk-and-ambush predator, the cougar pursues a wide variety of prey. Primary food sources include such ungulates as deer, elk, moose, and bighorn sheep, as well as domestic cattle, horses, and sheep."

"Well it has lots of deer where it lives that's for sure," Dylan said.

"Look at this: This cat prefers habitats with dense underbrush and rocky areas for stalking and for concealment." "That's exactly what he has up in the valley, brush, deer, and rocky cliffs."

Aidan looked at his friend. "This is amazing. There's a freaking cougar in our valley!"

"A what?"

The two boys looked up and there stood Clifford leering at them.

"What are you two girls whispering about, what's that bull crap about a cougar?"

Dylan stood up and stepped up to Clifford. "The reason we're speaking quietly is that we don't want some dope like you hearing what we're talking about you mutt. Don't you know it's not polite to eavesdrop?"

"This is a free library, I can stand wherever I like."

"Beat it Clifford or I'll take you outside and give you another lesson like I did back in 7th grade."

Clifford glared at him but backed down. "I don't care what you two girls are talking about anyway, I was leaving anyway."

He turned and stomped off to the other end of the library.

"What is it with that guy?" Aidan asked.

Dylan shrugged.

"He's got it out for you. What are you talking about that happened in 7th grade?"

"I'll tell you later, let's get back to this cougar stuff."

"Cougars are slender and agile members of the cat family. They are the fourth largest cats and adults stand about 2 to 2.5 feet tall at the shoulder. The length of an adult male is around 8 feet nose to tail and of this about 36 inches is tail. Males typically weigh between 115 and 220 pounds and females between 65 and 140 pounds." "Wow, that's a big kitty," Aidan said.

He continued, "The head of the cat is round and the ears erect. Its powerful forequarters, neck, and jaw serve to grasp and hold large prey. It has five retractable claws on its forepaws, (one a dewclaw) and four on its hind paws. The larger feet and claws are adaptations for clutching prey."

"Look at this, 'Cougars are not typically classified among the "big cats" as it cannot roar, lacking specialized larynx and hyoid apparatus of the *Panthera*. Like domestic cars, cougars vocalize low-pitched hisses, growls, and purrs, as well as chirps and whistles.'"

"So in those movies of a cougar roaring at the cowboy, it's all Hollywood," Dylan said.

"It seems like that," Aidan answered.

"Look at this paw print," Dylan said.

There was an exact copy of the picture they'd taken in the woods. Aidan opened his phone and brought up the picture and it was exactly the same."

"Cougars have large paws and proportionately the largest hind legs in the cat family. This physique allows it great leaping and short-sprint ability. An exceptional vertical leap of 18 feet is reported for the cougar. Horizontal jumping capability from standing position is suggested anywhere from 20 to 40 feet. The cougar can run as fast as 35 to 45 miles per hour but is adapted for short powerful sprints rather than long chases."

"Holy smokes, maybe we're not safe going up there after all."

"Look here, this tells about it," Dylan said. "The cougar is a reclusive animal and usually avoids people. Attacks on humans remain very rare with only 19 reported events since 1890. The majority of these attacks were on juvenile boys. The thought being that boys get out into the woods and wilds more than girls and being smaller than adults, seemed like likely prey. There have been no attacks on full grown humans with the exception of a very few women, who, again are smaller and easier prey."

"So in over 100 years there've been just a few attacks. I think we're big enough to be considered adults in the eye of that cat, so we're probably not in too much danger. Still I think we should be careful."

Just then the bell rang for the end of the period. Aidan shut down the computer and they walked out to the hall to go to their next classes. "We're going to have to look at some more sites to see if we can figure out where this thing came from," Aidan said as they parted.

"Yeah, I agree. We want to be sure of what we're talking about before we tell anyone. Holy smokes Aidan, just think, there's a cougar in the Big Valley."

They were both smiling as they parted in the hallway.

 **Chapter 6**

The boys went to baseball practice after school and then home. They rode the bus and as Aidan got off he said to Dylan, "Want to take the 4 wheeler up to the valley and sit until dark?"

Dylan grinned. "Sure, I'll come over in a few minutes."

They left Sally home just as a precaution in case they did see the cat. They didn't want to take a chance that she'd go after it and become a casualty. They also thought they'd have a better chance of seeing it without a dog making a lot of noise.

They parked the vehicle just inside the narrows where the trail ran into the valley and walked along the hillside for about a hundred yards, and then hiked up onto the hill and sat in a clearing where they could see the whole valley.

"You think we'll see it?" Dylan asked quietly.

Aidan shrugged. "We'll find out I guess."

They sat for twenty minutes without either of them saying anything. Aidan then remembered what Dylan had said to Clifford about 7th grade.

"Hey Dyl, what did you mean when you reminded Clifford about what happened in 7th grade?"

Dylan looked kind of sad. "Remember that kid who moved to town that year? His name was Bernard. His parents came from the Czech Republic I think. They lived next door to my aunt Betty."

"Yeah, I remember him. He was kind of a big kid, pretty quiet."

"Yeah, he was a big boy and they were dirt poor. He wore bibbed overalls and only had two or three shirts. He was always clean but he didn't have much. Remember he used to carry a plastic ice cream pail with his lunch? They couldn't afford for him to eat at school lunch so he brought sandwiches from home. He even had a glass jar with milk from home because they couldn't afford milk at school."

"Jeez, I didn't know that. I guess I never got to know him very well," Aidan said.

"Well, I did know him kind of well I guess. I was having a heck of a time with algebra and those dang story problems. One day I was in the library and was trying to figure one of them out and he sat near me. I saw him looking at my paper. He smiled and said something about those problems being fun, so I asked him to help me. He was really smart. In no time he helped me figure out how to solve those dang things and I kind of got to like him. He really didn't have any other friends I guess."

"How does Clifford fit in?"

"Well one day Bernard was all upset and the pocket on his shirt was torn so I asked him what happened. He said it was nothing but I saw Clifford and some of the other dopes laughing so I put two and two together. A couple of days later I was leaving school late. I think you'd gone home already but I had something late. When I came out the door there was Clifford sitting on top of Bernard on the lawn, slapping him. He'd taken Bernard's lunch pail and dumped it on the ground and broken his milk jar. I was so pissed I ran over and grabbed Clifford by the collar on his shirt and jerked him off Bernard and punched him in the nose. He got up and came at me and I flattened him and he went down again. I was so angry that I told him if he got up again I was going to beat him to death."

"Holy shit, I never knew that. Why didn't you tell me?"

"Bernard was so embarrassed at being picked on that I said I'd keep it a secret. But I told Clifford that if he ever said anything about it or ever touched Bernard again I'd take him out and beat him till he couldn't walk."

"Wow, no wonder he hates you."

Dylan shrugged. "It made me so mad. Bernard didn't hurt anyone. He was just a kid who was overweight and poor and that was why a bully like Clifford chose him as his victim. Well afterward I helped Bernard up and brushed him off and walked home with him. When we got there he begged me to come in, so I did. His mom was a big lady too and when Bernard told her what I did she hugged me and cried and thanked me for helping him. Jeez I felt so bad."

"Dyl, that was awesome what you did," Aidan said.

"I didn't do much but she thought it was so great. Anyway she made me sit down and gave me a glass of milk and some cookies and we sat and talked and they were really nice people. From then on I kind of watched out for Bernard and his mom always thanked me when she saw me at school or up town."

"You did good Dylan."

"It was really nothing. You remember that Bernard and his parents moved away the next year?"

"Yeah, I guess they did, but like I said I didn't know him very well."

"Well, that summer a year after they moved, I got a letter from his mom. They'd moved down by the Mississippi river someplace to a farm by Prairie du Chien. I guess Bernard got a job on a farm down the road and one day the farmer came to pick him up and on the way back they had a crash with the milk truck.......and Bernard was killed."

Aidan looked at his friend. "Oh no, he was only what....12 or 13?"

"He was 13, just turned. His mom thought I should know. And she told me that Bernard talked about his friend who lived in his old town all the time after they moved. She wanted me to know how much that little thing of sticking up for him meant to him."

Dylan's eyes were filled with tears and he turned his head

33

away from Aidan.

Aidan put his arm around his friend's neck. "Just think of how happy you made him just for being decent to him. Wow. That's something Dyl."

Dylan shrugged. "So now you see why Clifford hates me. And now you know why I torment him whenever I get the chance. I want to make his life as miserable as I can."

"Well if anyone deserves it, he sure as heck does."

It was now getting dark so they got up and walked back to the 4 wheeler. As they were getting on the vehicle Aidan smiled at his buddy. "Thanks for sharing that with me Dyl. I know it must have been hard to relive it."

"Yeah it was. I wish I could have done more for them all but who knows that something like that is gonna happen?"

"You're right. You never know. But I know one thing... I picked the right guy to be best friends with."

Dylan grinned. "Now if we can find that cougar and keep from getting eaten, we just might have a heck of an adventure."

"No foolin."

 **Chapter 7**

Aidan hadn't thought Wednesday morning was anything special when he got up. He'd forgotten it was his birthday and didn't realize it until he walked downstairs and saw Dylan sitting at the breakfast table with a birthday present in front of him. "Happy birthday my friend," he said as Aidan walked into the kitchen.

"Holy smokes I forgot all about it," Aidan said, "What with all the excitement with the cat and stuff."

"What cat?" his mom asked as she came from the pantry.

"Oh, just a cat that was up in the Big Valley mom. We were wondering where it came from."

"Those barn cats that go into the wild are bad critters," she said. "You know I heard that they're responsible for the deaths of hundreds of song birds every year. They shouldn't be in the woods."

"Well, we'll watch for this one and if we see it we'll try to catch it," Dylan said snickering.

The boys began working on a stack of pancakes and sausage and soon Aidan's father came in from the barn. He sat with the boys and ate with them. "So did you ever find that cooler?" he asked.

"Yeah we did, we went up on the hill and found it. It was all wrecked."

His dad looked interested. "What do you mean all

wrecked?"

Aidan looked at Dylan and he nodded. "Dad, can you keep a secret?"

"Well I guess....it depends on what it is."

"Dad, there's a cougar living up in the Big Valley."

Aidan expected his father to be surprised and not believe him but he looked at the boys and nodded his head. "I've heard rumors of a big cat around here for a while now. If that's where he's living, I'm not surprised."

"You've heard rumors? What kind of rumors are you talking about?"

"Well there's been talk in town and at the Feed Mill. It seems that the UPS man saw what he thought was a cougar last autumn. Everyone kind of made a joke of it but then Mrs. Storms from up the road a little way......she claims she saw it last spring too."

"Holy cow, so it's true?"

His dad shrugged. "There are those who think it could be and those who think these folks saw something and mistook what it was. What makes you guys think this is a cougar?"

Aidan opened his phone and punched a couple of buttons and turned it to his dad. He took the phone from Aidan and reached into his pocket for his reading glasses. He looked carefully at the picture of Dylan's hand next to the paw print in the dirt. He raised his eyebrows. "Wow, that's pretty convincing, you guys saw this up in the valley?"

Aidan nodded. "Just a few feet from the cooler that was all wrecked and what was left of our fish stringer."

"Hmm. So what are you two thinking of doing?"

Dylan smiled and lifted up the package he'd brought for Aidan's birthday present. "Open this and I think that it'll be a good idea."

Aidan opened the package and it was a trail camera. "Oh man this is perfect. We can set it up by the cliffs and if he goes past, we'll have proof that he's there," Aidan said. "Jeez Dyl that's a great present, thanks."

"You're welcome I thought it was just what we needed to get a look at this big kitty."

"You guys take care messing with that thing," his dad said. "I'm not sure how one would act if you got too close so don't take any stupid chances."

"Dad, you must have us confused with some other stupid teenagers," Aidan said.

The boys headed up to the road to wait for the bus and while they stood there Dylan said, "If we win the game tonight we'll be playing Saturday but if we lose tonight we're done for the year. Either way let's get that camera up in the woods as soon as we can."

"Yeah, I agree. Can you drive me to my driver's test Friday after school?"

"Sure, what car are you going to use?"

"I'm taking mom's car. I've been practice driving in it and it's smaller so it's easier to parallel park."

"Good idea. You could use our pickup but it's a tank and you'd probably flunk in it."

They got on the bus and rode to school. When school was over they got their uniforms on and played their last baseball game of the season. The other team got off to a big lead with Clifford pitching and by the 4th inning the coach took him out and replaced him with Dylan. By the time Dylan got in the lead was too big and they didn't catch up by the last inning. On the way into the school after the game Clifford walked past them and glared at Dylan. "I had everything under control Mahoney. We didn't need you to screw up the last innings."

Dylan looked surprised. "You had it under control? They batted around the whole lineup in the second inning and scored 5 runs you dope. If we'd have left you on the bench the whole game we might have had a chance but the coach felt sorry for you loser."

Clifford stopped and turned to Dylan.

Dylan stepped up to him and got nose to nose with him. "Go ahead Clifford, I'm not slow and I'm not scared like Bernard was. Go ahead and I'll give you a couple more black eyes."

"What's going on?"

They turned and the coach was coming across the field. "Nothing coach, Clifford had something in his eye and I was seeing if I could spot it."

Clifford scowled and turned toward the school. "One of these days Mahoney, one of these days," he said as he stomped off.

Dylan grinned at Aidan who was catching up to him. "You better think twice about hanging with me Aidan, I'm on Clifford's list."

"Oooh, I'm shaking in my cleats," Aidan laughed.

Chapter 8

"Are you nervous" Dylan asked as Aidan drove into town and pulled into the parking lot of the driver's licensing building.

"A little, but I think I know enough to pass. If a dope like you can pass I sure can," he said grinning.

They walked in and Aidan stood in line and when it was his turn he got a clipboard filled with papers to fill out and then left with a lady to take his road test. Dylan picked up a magazine and paged through it while Aidan was gone.

In about twenty minutes Aidan returned and had a grin on his face. He gave Dylan a thumbs up and walked up to the area where they took the picture for the license, got his picture taken and then came to sit by Dylan and wait for the license to be processed.

"I only missed four points," he said. "I scraped the curb a little parallel parking but that was about all I did wrong."

Dylan nodded. "I did that too, that's the scariest part I think."

A short time later Aidan picked up his brand new license and they headed back home. "Now all I have to do is talk my parents into buying a car for me," he said.

"Good luck with that!"

"Well, I think we should celebrate," Aidan said when they got to his house. "Let's put some food together and to up to the valley and camp tonight. If we have time we can put the trail cam up and if not we can do it in the morning."

"Good idea," Dylan said.

They got Aidan's stuff together and loaded up Sally and the food in Aidan's dad's pickup and went to Dylan's house, got his stuff and took the 4 wheeler back into the valley.

Sally galloped around letting off steam while the boys put

things away. "Let's go up and put that camera on the trail up by the cliffs," Aidan said.

They hiked up the hill and found a perfect tree right off the trail and strapped the camera to it. Dylan opened the waterproof case and pressed a button to activate the thing and then they closed it up and hiked back down to the valley.

"Well, we'll see in the morning if anything walked down that trail, then maybe we'll have proof of the cat."

They settled into their lawn chairs at the edge of the pond and fished until dusk. Since they only had one small trout, they decided on eating hot dogs and chips for supper. When they were finished they sat under the stars and talked.

"What are we going to do if we do get a picture of the cat?" Dylan asked.

"I don't know. I think we should keep it quiet. If we tell too many people somebody will surely come up here and try to see it or maybe even shoot it."

"I wonder if it's legal to shoot a cougar in Wisconsin?"

"I don't know. I suppose it's like that elk a few years ago. Theoretically there are no cougars in Wisconsin, so I don't know how it could be illegal to shoot something that doesn't officially exist."

"That doesn't make sense, but I see what you mean," Dylan said. "I think it's kind of cool to think of a cougar being here, I'd hate to see someone harm it."

"Me too.....we'll see if we can prove it's here. Then we can go from there."

They decided to turn in for the night and crawled into the tent, stripped off their shoes and socks, jeans and tee shirts and got into their sleeping bags. Sally snuggled down in her spot and soon they were all sleeping.

The next thing Aidan knew the sun was shining on the tent, warming it up inside. He looked over at Dylan who was sleeping on his side with his arm around Sally. She was snoring quietly and he grinned at the two of them. He hated to disturb them but he had to pee badly, so he crawled out into the morning sun. Somewhere up on the hill a tom turkey was gobbling and a little way down the valley a hen yelped to answer him. Aidan did his business and crawled back into the tent.

"Was that a turkey gobbling?" Dylan asked.

"Yeah, first one I've heard gobble this spring. You know turkey season opens in a couple of weeks. We need to do some scouting so we know where to sit when our season gets here."

"Yeah, you're right. We can "turkey look" and "cougar look" at the same time."

Sally got up and crawled out through the open door and Aidan dressed and crawled out barefoot to begin breakfast. He heard Dylan rummaging around inside the tent and then he heard a loud fart from inside.

"Leave the tent flap open when you come out," he laughed.

"Wasn't me, it was Sally."

By the time Dylan had peed Aidan had bacon and eggs fried and piled onto paper plates. They sat in their lawn chairs and ate and enjoyed the warm spring morning. "Let's finish up and then hike up and see if we got any pictures," Dylan said.

"I've been thinking the same thing. What do you think? Think we got a picture of him?"

Dylan shrugged. "We'll soon see."

When they got to the trail cam they snapped open a clip on the strap that held it to the tree and took it down. Aidan opened the back and pulled out the digital camera inside. He pushed a couple of buttons to view the pictures. The first picture was just at dusk and it was of a raccoon. The next five pictures were of the same raccoon scrounging around in the leaves along the trail.

The next picture was of a small fork horn buck. There were three pictures of it, one coming from the hill, one right at the camera and one going away. The next picture was of something too close to the camera and they had nothing but a big brown blur, but the next was the tip of an animal's tail.

41

"Holy smokes... look at that!" Aidan said.

There was about ten inches of a tan colored round short haired tail with a black tip on the end. "That's a cougar tail if I ever saw one," Dylan said. "Look at the next one!"

Aidan clicked the button again and nothing came up. He clicked it once more and there was nothing. "That's it, no more."

He looked at Dylan. "It must have walked right past the camera, that's what that big brown blob was and the second shot was his tail as he passed."

"Well, we're not going to convince anyone with a blob and the end of a tail," Dylan said dejectedly.

Aidan grinned at his friend. "Well, I really didn't expect to get a magazine cover photo the first time out anyway. At least we know he's here."

"Yeah, you're right. Let's re-set it and leave it for a day or so. I'll bet next time we'll have something. At least we know it works."

Chapter 9

"We need to talk to those people who saw the cougar," Aidan said as they motored through the narrow gap in the hills that led them out of the valley. "I think we can watch for the UPS man at school. I've seen him drive up nearly every day during lunch break."

"Yeah, he usually is there about the same time each day. How about we drive up past Mrs. Storms' house and see if she's home. We can stop and talk to her and see what she has to say."

"Good idea, can you get your dad's pickup?"

"I think so, if not maybe you can, now that you have a license," Dylan answered.

"Oh yeah, I kind of forgot about that. I've had it such a short time that it didn't even cross my mind."

"What we need to do is get a car or pickup. If one of us has wheels we'll be in good shape."

They got home and Dylan's dad let them take the truck. Sally jumped up in the back and they got in and headed up the hill towards the Storms place. The farm was just up the road about a mile from the Big Valley and Mrs. Storms was in the yard planting flowers in a garden at the side of the house. They pulled in and got out of the truck and walked up to her.

"Good morning boys, what brings you around here?" she said wiping potting soil from her hands.

"Good morning," Aidan said, "I don't know if you know us. I'm Aidan Grant and this is Dylan Mahoney, we live down the road a little way. We've had some interesting experiences lately and we have an idea that there may be a cougar living in the valley on our farm. My dad said he'd heard that you might have seen a big cat?"

She smiled. "So that's where he went. Yes, I've seen him. It was about a year ago, when my husband was still alive. He was pretty weak with cancer and I was spending my time with him as much as I could. We had about a dozen calves in a pasture up on the hillside," she said pointing up the valley. "One morning I got up and the cattle were down by the barn, they'd broken out of their pasture. I went out to try to herd them back but they were just wild. They bawled and stamped and were really skittish, like they'd been scared half to death. So I asked my husband to help me and we got them back in the pasture. I took some wire up and fixed the fence where they'd broken out. A couple days later they were out again and just scared silly like before."

"But they weren't hurt?"

"No there was nothing wrong with them except they were scared to death. Well this happened four more times in the next couple of weeks. We couldn't figure out what was scaring them. Then one morning I went down by the barn to feed my horses. I had three of them and two colts. While I was feeding them they began to whinny and stamp and suddenly they all stampeded right at me. I was by the feed bunk and jumped behind it or they'd have trampled me. They were really gentle so they weren't after me. They were running away from something that had scared them."

"Holy smokes, "Dylan said.

"Well I knew there was something going on but had no idea what it was. You know once and a while someone thinks they see a bear in these parts, so I thought it may be that but no one had seen anything. Anyway a couple of days later my husband was hungry for bacon. When you have cancer one of the things that really are hard is to eat. They have no appetite so when he said he was hungry for bacon I said I'd run to town and get some. I jumped in the car and started down the road and right up there," she said pointing to a curve in the highway, "I was going around that curve and looked to the left and standing up about half way across that field was a cougar. I stopped and it stopped walking and turned and looked at me. It stood there for a couple of minutes and then turned and walked up into the woods."

"You're positive it was a cougar."

She smiled. "I may be getting old boys, but I can still see pretty well and I know a cougar from a barn cat or a lynx or bobcat. This thing was about 7 or 8 feet long from nose to tail. The tail was probably about 3 feet long. It was tan, had small tight ears, very powerful front legs and paws. It was definitely a cougar."

"Did you ever see it again?" Aidan asked.

"No I never did. Our cattle settled down and we never had any problems with it since. Our neighbor and his wife were up on that ridge last fall picking corn and they saw it cross the picked field. They told me because I'd told them that I'd seen it. They wanted to let me know that I wasn't crazy after all."

The boys laughed. Dylan looked at Aidan. "You know what's about ¾ of a mile the other side of that hill don't you?"

Aidan nodded. "The Big Valley," he said. He turned to Mrs. Storms. "You know that big long valley on our farm? We camp and hunt and fish up there a lot and we've been visited by something a couple of times and came to the conclusion that it's a cougar."

She smiled and nodded knowingly. "That'd be a perfect place for him to live. Its way back where there are no roads, the hills are steep and not many people go back there. It's no wonder that I've never seen him again, he found a good home and is probably staying right there."

"Yeah, that's what we thought too," Dylan said. "Well thank you for telling us about it. We weren't sure if we were imagining things or not but your story makes it pretty clear, we have a cougar living around here."

"I hope you guys aren't going to try to harm it. It's really quite an elegant thing... a really beautiful animal."

"Oh no, we don't want to hurt it. We just want to see it and keep others away from it so it can live in peace. We think it's very cool to have it here," Aidan said.

She smiled. "I think so too. Let me know if you find it. I'd like to hear how it's doing."

The boys promised to let her know and left. As they were driving down the road Aidan said, "Well, I've got little doubt now do you?"

Dylan shook his head. "If you can't believe a little old lady, you can't believe anyone. Dang Aidan, just think, there's a for real live cougar living right next to us. Holy smokes, how cool."

"We gotta be quiet about it though Dyl, if we let it out somebody is sure to mess with it and get hurt or hurt it."

Dylan nodded. "Mum's the word," he said.

 Chapter 10

Monday at school the boys agreed to meet outside the school office after the noon break to watch for the UPS man. They grabbed a couple of sandwiches from the cafeteria and sat on some benches waiting and hoping he'd get there before they had to go back to classes.

"Here he comes," Dylan said nodding toward the front door of the school.

The UPS man came in carrying three packages and went into the office to deliver them. They could see him talking to the secretary and soon he came out and headed toward the front door.

"Um, hey could we talk to you for a minute?" Aidan said walking quickly over to the man.

"Sure, what's up boys?"

"I'm Aidan Grant and this is Dylan Mahoney, we live up on Hwy Q. We heard that you saw something a while back that was unusual."

The man grinned. "You heard that hey? Well you heard right. My name is Tom by the way. Yeah last fall I was coming down that very road when I saw something in the grass beside the road. I figured it was a deer so I slowed down and then this cat stepped out into the road and stopped and looked right at me. I stepped on the brakes and sat there looking at the dang thing and I'll be danged if it wasn't a cougar. It stood there for a half a minute and then took a long leap and disappeared into the grass on the other side of the road."

"There was no doubt in your mind it was a cougar?" Dylan asked.

"No more doubt than I'm sure that you two guys are humans. It was a big beautiful cougar. The body was tan and he was probably 5 feet long not counting the tail. The tail was another three feet and had a black tip. It wasn't any barn cat it was a full grown cougar or mountain lion or puma, whichever you like."

The boys looked at each other and nodded.

"You boys have seen it?"

"Not really. On Aidan's farm there's a big long valley way back in the hills that is really secluded. He and I camp back there a lot and we've been visited a couple of times in the night by something that stole our cooler and our fish on a stringer. We set up a trail cam and got a picture of its tail.....round, tan with a black tip," Dylan said.

Tom smiled. "A big secluded valley, that's a perfect place for him to set up his home range. No wonder he hasn't been seen by anyone else except that Sheriff's Deputy."

"What Sheriff's Deputy?"

"His name is Biba, he lives up the road a little way from your place. I heard he saw it a while back."

Dylan looked at Aidan, "Another person for us to talk to," he said.

"I hope you guys aren't going to do anything stupid with that cat," Tom said. "I don't think he'd bother you but if you corner it you might be in trouble."

"Oh don't worry we're not going to mess with it. We'd just like to see it and then hopefully no one will find out about it and it can live its life in peace," Aidan said.

"That sounds like a good idea," Tom said. "Well good hunting guys."

Tom walked back to his big brown truck and drove off. "Wow, this is something huh?" Aidan said.

"What're you dopes sneaking around about talking to the UPS guy about?"

They turned and there stood Clifford and Sonny smirking.

"None of your business and don't you know it's not polite to eaves drop?"

"We were just enjoying the sunshine. We didn't hear anything."

Dylan walked up to Clifford. "Listen you stay away from us and you stay away from our farms. We catch you sneaking around on our land and we'll call the Sheriff and have you arrested for trespassing."

"Don't threaten me," Clifford said. "We have a right to hunt and fish anywhere we like."

"Not on private property you don't," Dylan said.

"Dylan, let it go," Aidan said.

Dylan stood there and then turned and walked away. He and Aidan went into the school and Aidan said, "Don't say anything about the valley. If they think we're hiding something up there, that's the first place they'll try to sneak into."

"Yeah, that was stupid of me," Dylan said. "I just get so tired of Clifford thinking he can push me around. I guess one of these days I'm going to have to remind him that he's not as tough as he thinks he is."

"Well, let's hope it doesn't come to that but if it does, I'll have my money on you."

Chapter 11

"I'm getting pretty tired of Mahoney telling me what to do," Clifford growled to his pal Sonny. "He thinks he can push me around but I'm not going to take it much longer."

"What were they talking about a cat?"

"I'm not sure, but I think they saw something up in that valley they think is all theirs. I thought I heard something about a cougar."

Sonny laughed. "A cougar... where do they think we live... Colorado?"

"That's what they were talking about with the UPS guy. I heard him telling something about something crossing the road. You suppose there really is a cougar up there someplace?"

"Will you listen to yourself? There aren't any cougars in Wisconsin. You must have heard wrong."

Clifford stared at Sonny. "I heard what I heard."

"Well, let's go up there and take a look," Sonny said.

"There's only one way into that valley and it's on Grant's land. We'd have to cross their pasture from the road to get in there. What if they catch us?"

"So what? What are they going to do have us arrested? We can just act like we didn't know it was private land."

Clifford shrugged. "Ok, lets get our dirt bikes and ride up there after school."

A few hours later the two of them turned off the highway on a little path that Aidan and Dylan had made with the 4 wheeler and followed it across the pasture and to the narrow opening that led into the Big Valley. They pulled up and stopped just outside the opening. "This is where they go in and out," Clifford said.

"Well, let's take a look see," Sonny said.

They fired up the bikes and rode through the opening along

the creek and soon were in the valley. They spotted the boys' tent and rode up to it. "Nice little spot they got here," Clifford said getting off his bike.

Sonny zipped the tent open and crawled inside. "Hey they got lots of stuff here, sleeping bags, pots and pans. We could help ourselves."

"We don't need any sleeping bags," Clifford said.

Sonny crawled back out. "So what do we do?"

Clifford stood looking out over the valley. "I don't know, we better get out of here in case they come out here. I just wanted to see what's in here."

"Maybe we should mess up their camp a little," Sonny said.

"They'd know it was us right away," Clifford said shaking his head.

"Yeah, probably so," Sonny said.

They poked around for a little longer and then got on their bikes and started down the trail to the opening in the hills. Suddenly Clifford pulled up and stopped his bike. "What're you doing?" Sonny asked.

Clifford walked over a fence next to the woods and pointed to it. "I just had an idea that might make an impression on those two. Maybe they'll get the idea that it's not a good idea to push me around any more.

Sonny looked at what Clifford was pointing to and a frown formed on his face. "You're not thinking what I think you're thinking are you?"

Clifford grinned. "It depends on what you think I'm thinking. I'm thinking we stretch this across the opening in the hills where the trail into the valley is and knock Grant and Mahoney off their 4 wheeler next time they come into their precious valley."

"Jeez, we might kill them. What if they're going real fast, we'd cut their heads off?"

"Oh don't be such a worry wart. They have to slow down to go through that narrow gap in the rocks. We'll just knock them on their butts and scare the crap out of them."

"I don't know," Sonny said.

"Are you gonna woos out on me? Come on give me a hand with this wire."

They rolled up several feet of loose wire from the fence that had been broken and left behind when the fence was repaired and then carried it on Clifford's bike back to the gap in the hill. Clifford wrapped one end around a medium sized tree on the right side of the opening and then stretched the wire across the gap to the other side where he wrapped it around another tree.

"There, that'll catch them about mid-chest. We'll see how they like that," he said.

Sonny just shook his head. "I don't think this is a very good idea Clifford."

"I don't care what you think dummy. Just keep your mouth shut when they come asking about it."

They got on their bikes and rode out of the gap to the highway and back to town.

Chapter 12

"Let's take a drive up to the valley and see if we've got anything new on the trail camera," Dylan said as he and Aidan got onto the school bus. "We can sit and watch for a while and see where the turkeys are working too."

"Good idea, it's not very long now until turkey season and we really should be thinking of where we're gonna hunt. We'll have to leave Sally home though," he said, "and you know how that's going to go over."

Dylan grinned. "You've let the dog take over," he said. "She pouts and you give in to her."

Aidan shrugged. "You've seen those big brown eyes. She looks so hurt... it's hard to say no."

Dylan just shook his head.

They got to Dylan's house and both of them got off the bus. Dylan changed into some camouflage clothes and they got onto the 4 wheeler and drove across the fields to Aidan's house. He ran in to change and Sally galloped around the front yard excited to see camouflage clothes, which to her meant they were going hunting.

Aidan came out of the house and she jumped up on the back of the vehicle. "Oh Sal, I'm sorry girl, you can't go today," he said. Sally sat there looking at him. "Come on Sal, get down, you can't go."

The dog's head dropped down and she slowly crawled off the vehicle and walked a short way away, her tail between her legs.

"Oh jeez," Dylan said. "Let's go or I'll change my mind before you do."

Aidan stooped over and hugged the dog. "You're a good girl, but you have to stay home this time."

He got on the back of the 4 wheeler and they drove off

without looking back.

"See what I mean?" he said into Dylan's ear as they sped across the field. "She makes you feel like you're a criminal if you leave her."

Dylan grinned. "You're too soft, but I have to admit she does know how to get her way most of the time."

A few minutes later they came to the back of the line of hills that bordered the big valley. Dylan slowed down when they got on the dirt trail that led through the narrow pass into the valley. "Look at those tracks," he said over his shoulder.

Aidan leaned to the side and looked at the tracks that had been made by the dirt bikes. "Dirt bikes, you think that dope Clifford's been up here messing around?"

"I don't know but I wouldn't put it past him. We better check our camp first."

Dylan slowed a little as they got to the gap in the rocks. Aidan was looking up on the hillside thinking that maybe he'd get a glimpse of the cougar when Dylan let out a shout.

Suddenly Aidan felt Dylan slam into him and the next thing he knew they were both laying on their backs on the dirt trail. The vehicle went on a few feet and slammed into a rock just as the kill switch shut it down. The vehicle was equipped with a switch under the driver's seat that shut it down if the driver got up or fell off the seat.

"What the heck?" Aidan said. "What did you do?"

Dylan was half way lying on Aidan's lap. He was clutching his right forearm and rolling from side to side. "Got knocked off!" he gasped. "My arm, I think it's broke."

Aidan slid out from under Dylan and laid him back on the ground. Dylan's right forearm was bleeding through his long sleeved shirt. "What the heck happened?" he asked.

"There was something across the trail, I saw it just in time to put my arm up or it would have taken my head off. Oh man, my arm!" he said, tears streaming down his face.

"Hold still as you can," Aidan said. He could tell something was very wrong because Dylan was a tough guy and it took a lot to make him cry.

"I'm gonna see if the 4 wheeler is ok and then we'll get you loaded up and to the hospital."

Aidan walked to the 4 wheeler and got on it. Everything looked ok, so he turned the key and it started right up. He backed it off the rocks and turned it around. Then he saw the barbed wire stretched across the path. "That dirty shit," he said to himself.

He stopped next to Dylan and shut the machine off. "Can you sit up?" he asked.

Dylan nodded. "With a little help I think I can," he said.

Aidan took Dylan's shoulders and helped him to a sitting position. Then he pulled his long sleeved tee shirt off over his head and wrapped it around Dylan's chest, immobilizing his arm. "There that should keep you from hurting it any more," he said.

Dylan nodded. "Did you see what we hit?" he asked.

"Someone stretched a length of barbed wire across the trail."

"Are you kidding me? It's a good thing I saw it at the last minute or might have broken my neck. Clifford's going to pay for this."

"We can't prove its Clifford but right now we need to get you to a doctor. I'll help you up."

Aidan helped Dylan to his feet and got him situated on the back of the vehicle. Then he got on and started it up and slowly drove back across the pasture and to the highway. Once they got on the highway it was smoother so he went a little faster. When they got to Dylan's house he ran inside. There was no one home, so Dylan told him where a spare set of keys for the pickup were and he got them and they loaded up and headed to town.

Aidan was going pretty fast around some of the sharp corners to town when Dylan said, 'You know I'm not going to die from this arm but if you slam this truck into a tree I might."

Aidan looked over at his best friend's grin. He slowed down.

"Sorry I got a little carried away."

They got to the clinic in town and thankfully there was a doctor on duty who took Dylan right into the examining room. Aidan went to the front counter to fill out the forms as best he could. The receptionist called a cell number that Dylan gave her for his mom and got hold of her. She soon arrived.

A while later the doctor came out of the room. "His right ulna is broken," he said. "That's the small bone in the lower arm. He has a pretty good gash just above his elbow from where the wire hit him also."

"But he'll be ok?" Aidan said.

"He'll be fine. We're going to wrap the arm and put on a temporary splint now. We can't put a cast on until the cut heals. He'll have some pain for a few days but he should heal nicely. That was a good idea to immobilize the arm with your shirt," he said handing Aidan the shirt. "Normally we have a No Shirt, No Service rule but in this case, we made an exception.

Aidan grinned as he pulled his shirt over his head. "Can I go and see him?"

The doctor nodded and then said to Dylan's mom. "He'll be ready to go in a few minutes... I'll get some prescriptions ready. He'll need some antibiotics and some pain pills."

The doctor and his mom left and Aidan walked into the exam room. Dylan was sitting there and a nurse was wrapping his arm. His long sleeved shirt was lying on the table. "So I guess you'll live," Aidan said.

Dylan grinned, "Yeah, but I'm not so sure about Clifford."

Chapter 13

Aidan was walking up to the front door of the school the next day when suddenly Sonny appeared. Aidan stopped and looked at Sonny. "You looking for me?" he asked.

Sonny looked nervous. "I heard Dylan got hurt," he said.

"Yeah he did, he broke his right arm," Aidan said.

Sonny looked miserable. "Did he get in a wreck or something?

"You know as well as I do what happened," Aidan said. "And if there's some way we can prove it, you and that dope Clifford are going to jail."

"It wasn't my idea," Sonny said. "I told him not to but he thought it would be funny."

"Funny? If Dylan hadn't seen the wire at the last minute he might have broken his neck. That's funny?"

"Jeez, I'm sorry Aidan, I should have stopped him, I..."

"You better tell that to Dylan, not to me," Aidan said and turned and walked into the school.

When he got to his locker he saw Clifford stop Sonny as he walked down the hall. They were talking close and Clifford suddenly turned and looked at Aidan and then back at Sonny. Aidan smiled and nodded his head. "Let Clifford sweat for a while," he thought.

After school he got off the bus and changed and jumped on his 4 wheeler and drove over to Dylan's house. Dylan was sitting in his dad's recliner, his injured arm carefully sitting on a pillow on the arm of the chair.

"You look like you're doing a little better," Aidan said noting the TV tray next to Dylan with a soda, chips, cookies and a sandwich on it.

Dylan grinned and nodded. "It's good to be an invalid," he

said. "My arm doesn't hurt much as long as I take my pain pills on time and Mom hovers over me making sure I have no needs."

"I had a talk with Sonny," Aidan said. "It was them. He said it was Clifford's idea and I pretty much believe him. I don't know if we can do anything about it or not."

"I've thought about it and I think it'd be better just to let it go for now and someday we'll get the chance to make Clifford pay. In the meantime he'll sweat for a while worrying about it."

Aidan grinned. "I think that's a good idea. So it's not so bad?" he said indicating Dylan's arm.

"Not too bad as long as I take my pain pill on time. I'm not going to be doing much with it for a while but I hope once they get the cast on it I'll still be able to go turkey hunting."

"We've got a couple of weeks till then," Aidan said. "I was thinking I'll go up to the valley and do a little "turkey looking" this afternoon. Maybe I can see where they're going to roost."

"Good idea. I think I'll sit here and enjoy being king."

"See ya later, your Highness."

Aidan went home and changed into his camouflage pants and shirt and grabbed a head net and hat. We fired up the 4 wheeler and drove up to the valley. When he got to the gap in the hills he stopped and got off and unwound the wire from around the trees it was attached to and rolled it up and put it onto the luggage carrier on the vehicle. Then he drove to their campsite and parked the 4 wheeler.

Aidan stood looking up the valley and finally decided on a spot that he thought might be a good place to see some turkeys. He hiked along the valley for a ways and then climbed up onto the side of the hill near an area that had a lot of oak trees. There were always acorns on the ground around those trees and he knew that turkeys loved acorns. He thought it would be as good a place as any to see some birds.

He picked a spot near an old treetop that had blown down the previous spring and cleared off the ground and sat down. Once he was situated he pulled his head net over his head and put his hat on.

There wasn't anything moving for nearly half an hour. Then he heard leaves crunching but knew from the sound it wasn't a turkey. Soon a big red squirrel came bounding along and stopped a few trees away and picked up an acorn. He gnawed on it and soon had it open. He ate the insides and picked up another. Aidan was enjoying watching the squirrel when he heard a "yelp, yelp" sound from further down the hillside. The squirrel looked up at the sound and then went back to his business. Aidan knew that was the sound of a hen turkey calling to her friends.

He concentrated on the hillside and soon heard another hen call followed by an answer from another farther up the hill. A moment later he saw movement and could see one of the hens coming through the brush. It didn't take long and there was movement all over the place as the flock of birds quietly appeared from the brush. Each bird would scratch and pick and then stop and hold her head up, looking and listening for danger. Once convinced that it was safe to keep going she'd scratch a bit and then pick some more.

Turkeys were often called the smartest birds in the woods, but Aidan didn't think that was accurate. Turkeys were the most careful birds in the woods. They watched and listened all the time and when there was a flock of them together, it was almost impossible for a predator to get close. Aidan smiled as he watched them work closer and closer.

As they worked their way through the woods the birds made little peeps and chirps, keeping track of each other and probably telling each other that all was well.

The birds were all around him pecking and scratching when suddenly one hen raised her head and made a different noise. "Putt, putt," she said. Instantly all of the bird's heads came up alert. Something was wrong. The "putt" sound meant danger but Aidan couldn't see anything amiss.

Aidan tried to look out the corner of his eye to see what had disturbed the first bird. She was standing tall and still as a stone. He couldn't see anything wrong but there surely was something making the birds nervous. He turned his eyes back to the other birds and suddenly there came the sound of brush cracking and all of the turkeys began putting and running in different directions. Two birds flew up into the trees, knocking down sticks and branches as they crashed through them. Out of the tall grass next to a brush pile there was movement. Aidan's mouth dropped open when the cougar sprang up out of the grass and grabbed a turkey that was about three feet off the ground trying to fly up into the trees for safety.

The bird's wings beat furiously and the cat brought the bird to the ground and chomped down on its neck and held it down with its front paws. The bird flapped for a minute and then was quiet. The cat picked it up and looked around the hillside holding the turkey in his mouth. Then he began walking quickly down the hillside toward the rocky cliffs.

Aidan sat there for a minute not sure he believed what he'd just seen. "Holy smokes," he said as he got stiffly to his feet, "I don't believe I saw that."

"You can believe it, because I saw it too." A voice came behind him.

Aidan jumped and turned toward the tree top. "What the heck?"

Suddenly a man covered in camouflage that had what looked like oak leaves sewed onto it stood up. "Sorry to scare you like that," he said.

"Scare me I almost crapped my pants! After seeing that cougar I was a little tense and then you spoke, holy cats, my heart is beating like a drum."

The man smiled and stepped forward.

 **Chapter 14**

"How did you get back there?" Aidan asked.

"I was sitting there when you came along earlier. I didn't see any reason to show myself and cause a lot of noise by talking so I just sat still to watch."

The man had only been ten feet from Aidan and he hadn't had a clue he was there.

The man pulled off one of his camouflage gloves and stepped forward. "I'm Mike Florian," he said extending his hand. "I own that farm at the end of the valley that borders your land."

"I'm Aidan Grant. Pleased to meet you," Aidan said. "I knew somebody owned that old farm but I didn't know you lived there."

"I come and go," Mike said. "I travel a lot. I suppose that's your tent down by the pond?"

Aidan nodded. "Yeah my friend Dylan and I camp there a lot. We put the tent up in the spring and leave it all summer. A while back something visited us during the night and stole a stringer of fish that we'd left in the water. That's what got us thinking there might be a critter in this valley that was not something you see every day."

Mike smiled. "Spirit likes fish. I've watched him fish along the creek several times. He's darn good at it too. He crouches down near the bank and waits for a trout to swim past. He's really quick, like all cats. He can grab a fish out of the water quicker than you can spit."

"You call him Spirit?"

"Yeah, he's like a ghost. Another name for ghost is spirit. I thought it was kind of appropriate."

"You've seen him a lot of times?" Aidan asked.

"I saw him the first time almost three years ago. As I said

I've owned the property for a while but didn't come up here much. I was out doing just what you were doing today, looking at turkeys when I saw him the first time. I've seen him off and on for the last three years but more consistently for the last six months or so. I think he's settled in and made this his territory now."

"I didn't know you were ever around here," Aidan said.

"Actually I talked to your father back when I bought the place and he said he had no problem with me coming into the valley to hunt or fish. I suppose since I wasn't around much, he probably never mentioned it to you."

"Oh it's no problem. You own part of the valley….it was just a surprise to me," Aidan said looking the man over. He appeared to be in his mid to late thirties. He was a big man, about six feet tall, well built and looked like he spent a lot of time outdoors. His hair was dark with a few gray hairs in it and he had friendly blue eyes. "So what do you do for a living?" Aidan asked.

"Well, it's kind of a long story," he said, "but I guess if I had to narrow it down I'd say I'm a writer. I write books."

"Wow, really? What kind of books?"

"Well that's just it. I write mostly outdoor books. I've written some outdoor humor, adventures and some non-fiction wildlife studies. I'm a biologist by training."

"So you make your living writing stories? That's pretty cool."

"Well just because you write a few books it doesn't make you a millionaire. If you happen to write one that sells a lot of copies you might make a lot but it depends on the books and how many you sell. But yeah, I make a pretty decent living and it's nice to be able to live like I do and not have to answer to anyone…well except my publisher when he's looking for a manuscript for a deadline at the printer."

"Are you writing about that cougar?"

"I'm working on a book about the lives of cougars but it was started before I found this one. He'll add nicely to the book but much of it is about cougars in places where they normally live....not Wisconsin."

"This isn't where cougars normally live?"

Mike smiled. "No, cougars once lived all over the United States but as the eastern part of the country was settled they were driven out or killed off. The main population is in the west, namely the Dakotas, Wyoming, Montana and up into Canada and down into Mexico. Even in places where there are suppose to be cougars, they're very seldom seen. They're very secretive. Plus they each have their own territory which can be many square miles, so they're not concentrated."

"What made him come here?"

"When a female cougar has babies she keeps them with her for the first two years. She teaches them to stalk prey and to hunt and kill. Then when they're all grown up and she's taught them everything they need to survive, she kicks them out of her range. Young males are not welcomed by other cougars, especially older males so they travel looking for a place to call home. This guy wandered looking for a place to live and found this valley. It's perfect for him. It's large enough for him to have enough to eat, it's secluded so he doesn't get interfered with by many humans, and he has a place to hide when he needs to hide. Those cliffs up there make a great den and when the weather gets bad he's got a nice snug place to stay warm and dry. Normally they don't go as far as Wisconsin but there have been other cougars in Wisconsin and several other states in the mid-west over the years."

"When he came to out tent the other night, do you think we were in danger?" Aidan asked.

"Cougars would rather hide or run than fight. The thought is that they will attack a human if they are sick or injured and can't catch their normal prey. But the records show that almost all human attacks are on kids or women, small people. I doubt he'd have been real brave with a couple of strapping six foot tall teenagers like you guys. He just saw a chance for a fish dinner without much work, and took it."

"We weren't sure but it's good to know we're not in too much danger. We'd like to see him and kind of keep track of him without letting too many people know he's here. We're afraid someone will try to hurt him if they find out."

"The less people know about him the better," Mike said.

"Well, I'm glad we met," Aidan said. "I better start back home."

"It was nice to meet you too," Mike said. "Why don't you and your friend come up to my place this weekend. I'll show you some pictures of old Spirit that I've taken."

"That sounds cool. Dylan broke his arm the other day so he's kind of laid up right now but I'm sure he'll be up for a visit."

"Just watch for my driveway about half way down the hill that goes into town. There's a rusty old mailbox on the right and the driveway is filled with weeds and ruts. A lot of people think the place is abandoned which is how I like it. I don't get too many people trying to sell me stuff or get me to go to their church meetings that way."

Aidan grinned. "We'll be up Sat. See you then."

 **Chapter 15**

Dylan was sprawled in his dad's recliner with his right arm resting on a pillow, sleeping when Aidan opened the front door. He opened his eyes and grinned. "How did the turkey looking go?"

Aidan wiggled his eyebrows, "I saw him Dyl. I saw the cougar!"

Dylan sat up. "No kidding, what happened?"

Aidan told Dylan of the cat sneaking up on the turkey and how he hadn't seen it until it pounced.

"Holy smokes, those cats have to be the sneakiest critters in the world. Turkeys are so careful, they watch all the time. I can't believe he got close enough to catch one without them seeing him."

"He got right next to them. There were probably 7 or 8 turkeys, so that's a lot of eyeballs looking for danger. It was really amazing, but that's not all," Aidan said. "After the cat caught the turkey and ran off, I got another shock. There was a guy sitting not ten feet from me camouflaged all up watching the show too."

"Who was it?"

"The guy's name is Mike Florian, he's the guy who owns that old farm at the end of the valley."

"I didn't know anyone lived there," Dylan said.

"He comes and goes, is what he said. He's a writer. He writes books and is writing one about cougars right now. He invited us up to his place Sat."

"Cool, my arm is feeling a lot better today. It's not throbbing any more, so I don't have to take those pain pills. They made me goofy."

Aidan laughed. "They didn't have to do much to make *you*

goofy."

Dylan had his arm wrapped in the temporary cast and in a sling as they drove along the highway to Mike's place. "He said the driveway looks pretty abandoned," Aidan said slowing down as they got to about where he figured the place was. Suddenly they saw the driveway going up the hillside. It looked just like Mike had told them. It was growing wild with weeds and there were ruts in it from the rain. Aidan turned onto the driveway and they followed it to the top of the hill and then through a small plot of woods to the house.

"Don't look like much," Dylan commented as they pulled into the yard.

"He's got a nice vehicle though," Aidan said noting the new 4wheel drive pickup parked on the grass.

The house looked like a typical old farm house, two stories tall, boxy and weathered. They parked and got out just as Mike came out the front door. "Hey, welcome, come on in," he said.

Aidan walked up to Mike and shook hands and introduced Dylan, "Mike this is my best friend Dylan Mahoney, Dyl this is Mike Florian."

They shook hands left handed since Dylan's right arm was in the sling. "Looks like you had some bad luck," Mike said nodding at Dylan's sling.

"It's kind of a long story but a guy who had a beef with me thought it'd be funny to string a barbed wire across our trail and I hit it on my 4 wheeler. I was lucky....if I hadn't seen it I might have taken my head off."

"Is the guy still alive?" Mike said grinning.

"Not for long."

"I can imagine. Well come on in, I'll grab a couple of sodas for you."

The boys followed Mike inside and were quite surprised. The inside of the house was all remodeled and looked like a log cabin. The floors were all polished hardwood, the walls were varnished logs and the ceiling was lap boards that had been varnished to a shine. Against the end wall was a huge rock fireplace with several deer heads mounted above it.

"Wow, this is nice," Aidan said looking around.

"I'm getting it finished slowly but surely," Mike said. "Eventually the outside will have a half log siding too but it's a big job for one person."

"You did all of this by yourself?" Dylan asked.

"Yeah, I'm pretty handy. I just work on it when I have time. This has been in the works for 3 years. It's hard to tell how long it'll take me to finish."

Mike went to the kitchen and the boys sat on the couch. There was a coffee table with several magazines and books on it and a pile of mail. Dylan looked at the mail and pointed to Aidan, "Dr. Michael Florian," he said pointing to an envelope.

"Hmm, he didn't say anything about being a doctor, he said he's writer."

Just then Mike came in with some sodas and a bowl of chips.

"So you're a doctor too?" Aidan asked.

"I have two doctorate degrees but not in medicine. I have a doctorate in Biology and one in Chemistry and a master's degree in Geology. I guess I'm one of those over-educated people they talk about."

"Wow, I have a difficult time understanding high school chemistry," Dylan said.

Mike laughed. "I didn't start out to get a whole bunch of degrees. I actually wanted to be a veterinarian but had to take a lot of science classes for pre-vet. Once I got into them I kind of got interested and kept at it. It's kind of strange, all of that science and I end up writing for a living."

"That all kind of ties in with the books you write though doesn't it?"

"Yeah, it does," Mike said.

"So Aidan tells me that you said the cougar, his name is Spirit? He came here from South Dakota or someplace like that?" Dylan said.

"I'm not positive, but if we could get some hair or maybe some scat we could have the DNA checked and it most likely would match the South Dakota line of cougars. There have been a few other cats this far east of the Mississippi and they've matched the DNA of those cats. In April 2008 police shot and killed a cougar on the north side of Chicago. The DNA tests on that cat showed it was from the Black Hills cats, of South Dakota. There was a cougar near Spooner, Wisconsin in 2009 that was photographed and two different ones caught on trail cameras in Indiana in 2010. Those most likely were the same cat though. So this guy isn't the only one who came this way looking for a home."

"That's amazing. Yet so few people have seen them," Aidan said.

"I've been in the west looking for cougar for research projects," Mike said, "and even in places where there are suppose to be many of them, you very seldom see one. They're solitary animals, and very stealthy."

"Boy they have to be stealthy to sneak up on a turkey."

"That takes a lot of sneaking," Mike said. "Turkeys are the most skittish animals that are out there. Every couple of steps they take they stop to make sure somebody isn't trying to eat them."

"So what do you think this one is going to do?" Aidan asked.

"He's been around here pretty much all the time for the last half year. I think he's established this as his home range. He'll go out on short treks probably looking for a female or just checking things out now and then, but I think he intends to make this valley his home."

"Wow, that'd be cool," Dylan said.

"This is a perfect place for him, since so few people come into the valley, but I'm afraid someone will see him out on one of his visits and then he may have problems," Mike said.

"Well we can't keep him from going out, but we can keep other people from coming into the valley," Aidan said.

Chapter 16

That night, a mile north of the valley on the edge of a residential subdivision, the large cat hunted. There were many smells from the houses that attracted him.

The cat stopped and crouched down when the yard light came on. He stood very still in the shadows of the woods next to the house. The door opened and a small dog wearing a little blue sweater came running out into the yard.

"Go potty Missy," a voice said from just inside the house. A teenage girl stepped out and behind her a little dog. The little dog was wearing a rhinestone collar. She sprinted out across the grassy yard. The girl was talking on her cell phone and stepped back inside the door letting it close.

The little dog ran around the yard sniffing and snuffing at the smells she came across. The cat stayed still as a statue watching.

"Hurry up Missy, Mama wants to get back to her show," the girl said as she opened the door and stepped out.

The little dog squatted and peed in the grass and then scratched with her back legs to cover her pee spot. Then she began sniffing again and working her way around the yard. She moved into the edge of the woods scratching at something in the leaves and then came sniffing along closer and closer.

The cat stiffened as the little dog walked within a few feet of it, unaware of its presence.

"Missy, hurry up......Missy where are you sweetie?"

The dog stopped and looked at the house and then continued on her way. She went a little farther and then stopped and hunched up and pooped in the leaves. When she was done she turned and sniffed and then scratched leaves over her poop. Satisfied that all was well she began to explore a little farther along the edge of the yard. Suddenly she stopped and stood very still.

The cat was only six feet away in the brush waiting. The dog had obviously sensed its presence. The muscles in it's legs tensed and in a motion almost too fast to see it happen, it pounced and caught the little dog by the hind leg as it raced for the house.

The dog began to scream and yip as the predator bit down on its neck. The dog struggled for a few seconds and then went limp.

"Missy! Missy, what's wrong? Where are you?"

The girl came running into the yard and started screaming as she saw her little dog being carried by the cat.

The cat crouched down and snuck back deeper into the woods, the little dog's body limp in its jaws.

 Chapter 17

During the next week Aidan and Dylan went to see Mike every day after school. There was a steep ridge that ran out into the end of the valley from Mike's house that made a great spot to sit and watch for the cougar. Mike had seen it from this spot several times so the boys thought this was a good chance for them to really get a good look at it.

"This is the fourth day we've sat here," Dylan said, "I'm beginning to think that your cat is all in your head."

"My cat, why is it my cat now that we can't spot it?"

Dylan just grinned. "Yours and Mikes I guess then," he said.

They were sitting on a log that had been a big cottonwood tree until it was toppled in a summer storm a few years earlier. The log was three feet across so it made a nice seat for them. "Maybe he's out someplace looking for a female cat," Aidan said.

"If they're as scarce as Mikes says they are, he'll be looking for a long time."

They could see the entire length of the valley. The stream looked like a blue streak as it meandered through the middle of the valley until it got to the pond. Their tent and camping stuff were on the bank of the pond right where they'd left it. To their left along the other side of the north end of the valley where the two ridge lines met, were the rocks and caves. That's where Mike said he thought the cat spent it's time, especially in foul weather and in the winter.

"Look," Aidan said pointing to the pond. "There's a goose down there."

Dylan looked and then saw a Canada goose sitting in the cattails. "I bet she's on a nest," he said.

Aidan nodded.

Dylan motioned with his head, "There's her husband or his wife, hard to tell."

Aidan saw another goose with its wings set landing in the pond. The second goose settled onto the water, wagged its tail and began swimming into the cattails toward its mate.

"Cool, that's not something you see every day," Dylan said.

The boys watched the geese as the second one got to the nest. The two birds flapped their wings and their necks came up and they wrapped their necks around each other, something like a hug. Then the goose on the nest got up and stepped into the water. The other goose stepped up onto the nest and flapped its wings and then settled down on the clutch of eggs that were there.

Aidan looked at Dylan and grinned. "That was something to see wasn't it?"

Dylan nodded but looked concerned. "Something's in the cattails behind the goose," he whispered.

Aidan looked back farther and soon could see the shape also. "Oh my gosh.....I think that's the cat," he whispered. They were a hundred yards from the scene but it seemed like it was necessary to be very quiet. "Do you think he's going after the goose?"

"Looks like," Dylan said.

Aidan found he was holding his breath as the cat began to slowly move through the cattails. It was so slow he could hardly see any movement but the cat took tiny steps and moved inches at a time but got closer and closer to the nest.

"There's water in those cattails," Dylan said. "Do you think he'll get in the water?"

"I think cougars don't mind water. He's obviously hungry so I bet he will."

It seemed like it took forever but the cat was now only a few yards from the geese. The one on the nest was sitting quietly and the other was swimming around in the water eating some water plants. Suddenly the goose on the nest raised its head and began looking around. It began to honk and flap its wings and the other goose swam towards the nest its wings flapping and raising a heck of a fuss honking and hissing at the cat.

"They saw it or heard it," Dylan said.

Both geese now stood on the nest honking and flapping their wings, necks craned up looking very angry. The cat lay still as a stone.

Suddenly the cat stood up and the geese went wild. Instead of flying away to safety they held their ground protecting their eggs. The cat stood there its tail whipping back and forth as if it was making up its mind about attacking.

One of the geese actually started toward the cat, its wings held up above its head, honking like crazy.

"Oh oh, that's gonna make him attack," Dylan said grabbing Aidan's sleeve.

But instead of attacking the cat backed off a few feet. It stood there, tail twitching and then turned and slunk back toward the shore.

"Oh my gosh, do you believe that?" Aidan said turning to Dylan.

They watched as the cat got to the hard ground and then stood looking back at the geese for at least a minute. Then he started around the side of the pond toward the upper end of the valley. He got to the place where Mike had said he's seen him fishing and lay down on the creek bank.

"Oh no, he's going fishing now," Aidan said incredulously.

The boys watched as the cat lay on the bank of the creek looking down into the water. It didn't move a muscle but just watched the water. Ten minutes went by and the boys were relaxed and sitting back enjoying the scene when suddenly the cat grabbed down into the water with its right paw and scooped a nice brown trout up onto the grass. It grabbed the trout and put its front paws around the fish and began to eat it.

The boys looked at each other. "Do you know how lucky we are?" Dylan said.

"I bet there aren't three other people in the whole world who've seen what we saw today," Aidan answered.

They watched as the cat finished the fish, went to the edge of the stream and then sauntered up into the woods.

They got up from their log and stretched. "So do you doubt me now?" Aidan said.

"I'll never doubt you again," Dylan said smiling.

 Chapter 18

The boys were walking down the hallway to their lockers when they noticed a bunch of girls all clustered around one girl who was crying.

"Uh oh, that's a good place to stay away from," Dylan said grinning.

"Yeah, she probably broke a nail or some other tragedy," Aidan added.

They continued on to their lockers and got their books and went to class. Later at the lunch period they were sitting in the cafeteria eating their lunch with several friends when the same girls arrived in a group.

"Oh boy, there's Susie, the weeper," one of their friends whispered.

"What's she so upset about?" Dylan asked.

The boy laughed. "She says that some giant cat ate her little fifi dog last night."

Aidan looked at Dylan with alarm. "What do you mean a giant cat?"

The boy shrugged, "I don't know for sure, I wasn't going to ask and then have to hear the whole story with all that crying and stuff. From what I heard she let the little mutt out to pee and a giant cat grabbed it and took off with it."

"What kind of a dog was it?"

"I don't know, one of those little yappy things...... a Peekapoo or something like that.   Not like a real dog, like a retriever or something."

One of the other boys chimed in, "It was one of those little things that they put sweaters on and paint their toenails.   A complete waste of dog material if you ask me."

"Right," the first boy said, "If it can't retrieve a pheasant or tree a squirrel it's a waste of dog stuff."

Aidan looked at Dylan and gave him a warning look, so he'd keep quiet about the cat. Dylan understood and said nothing.

After they ate their lunch they hung around the hallway hoping to get the girl alone and ask her about her dog. Soon the gaggle of girls came down the hall and began to separate to their respective lockers. The bereaved girl began working on her lock as the boys walked up.

"Hey Susie, we heard you lost your dog?" Aidan said.

Susie turned to them. Her eyes were all red and she seemed on the verge of breaking down crying again. "Missy, her name was Missy. She was attacked by a big cat last night. We got flashlights and looked all over the woods and didn't find her." Susie's eyes filled with tears but she kept it together.

"Jeez, I'm sorry to hear that," Dylan said. "What do you mean a big cat? Was it like a huge tomcat?"

"It wasn't a regular cat! It was a big wild cat, it was huge."

Aidan knew they had to be careful. "Like how big was it?"

"I don't know how big for sure. I was on the phone and I heard Missy yelp and when I looked out the door I saw this cat with Missy in its jaws."

"Was it like this?" Aidan said holding his hands three feet apart.

"Bigger than that."

"How much bigger?"

"I don't know for sure. I only saw it for a second. It was a lot bigger than Missy."

"What color was its fur?" Dylan asked.

"It was dark I couldn't really tell," Susie answered.

"Hmm, that seems strange that there'd be a big cat like that... did you see if it had a long tail or a short tail?"

Susie thought for a second. "Hmm, you know I'm not sure. I was more looking at Missy in its jaws. It happened so fast, I really didn't see it really well."

"But you're sure it was a cat?"

"Oh yeah, I'm sure. It had a cat's face and cat's ears. It was a cat, a huge monster cat."

"Well we're sure sorry you lost your dog," Dylan said.

The boys walked back to their lockers. "What do you think?" Aidan asked.

"I think if our cat is out hunting people's dogs he's gonna get himself shot."

"We better go talk to Mike," Aidan said.

Chapter 19

Aidan and Dylan rode the school bus home and they both went to their respective houses and changed into after school clothes. Aidan waited on the front porch and soon Dylan came down the driveway in the family pickup and stopped. Aidan got in and they headed up to Mike's house to tell him about the cat killing the little dog.

"Boy I hope Susie's wrong," Dylan said.

"The problem is that she's saying it was a big cat, so people are going to hear that and everything that happens from now on will be blamed on a big cat."

"Yeah, you're probably right about that. But several people have seen the cat anyway, nothing ever came from that."

"Yeah but nobody's little dog got snatched either. If the cat starts killing dogs and maybe cattle, the crap is going to hit the fan," Aidan said.

They got to Mike's driveway and navigated up the steep rutted road and were relieved to see Mike's vehicle in the driveway by the house. They got out and went to the door and knocked but no one answered. "Not home," Dylan said.

"I bet he's down in the woods at his favorite lookout spot," Aidan said.

They walked down the trail to the end of the ridge and there was Mike sitting with his back against a big rock watching the valley.

"Hey guys," Mike said quietly.

"Hey Mike, have you seen him today?" Aidan asked.

"Not yet. I've been here for less than an hour."

The boys sat down in the grass. "Mike we might have a problem with the cat," Dylan said.

"What's that?"

"At school today one of the girls was carrying on about a big cat that ate her little dog last night. She claims it snatched the little critter right from their back yard."

Mike looked confused. "What time of day was it?"

"I'm not sure, but she said when it happened they went into the woods with flashlights to find the dog, so it must have been in the evening," Dylan said.

"I saw Spirit down in the valley about dusk yesterday. He had a young turkey in his mouth and he was heading up into the rocks, so I figure he took it up there and ate it."

"This was yesterday?" Dylan asked.

"Yeah, it was probably a bit after 6 o'clock. I remember thinking I was getting hungry, so I was just about to leave when I saw him. Where was this place that the dog got attacked?"

Dylan looked at Aidan. "Do you know where she lives?"

"I think it's off XX a little way. I know they live in the country but they don't farm, just live in a farmhouse."

"XX is two miles from here at least," Mike said.

"So what are you saying, he couldn't have done it?"

"I'm not saying that for sure but why would he travel two miles to eat a little dog when he had a turkey already caught?" Mike asked.

"You're right it wouldn't make much sense for him to kill again when he had plenty of food. They don't just kill for the fun of killing do they?"

"I've never heard of it happening," Mike said. "They kill to eat, I don't think they get any fun from it, it's just to stay alive."

"Maybe she just thought she saw a big cat," Dylan said.

"She seemed pretty sure of it though," Aidan replied.

"Well, we need to find out and to document when and where the cat is as much as we can," Mike said.

"How are we going to do that?"

"Well, we can watch as much as we have time for but we can also put out trail cameras all over the valley and document where he is and when."

"We have one camera out already," Dylan said.

"And how long is it since you checked it?"

"Oh um sure, it's been a while."

"I have half a dozen cameras at the house. I've used them in studies I've done on different species over the last few years. These are the newer ones too.....they have infrared on them as well as a regular camera. We need to get them set up around the valley and then check them for pictures regularly."

Dylan looked at Aidan. "I'm in, it sounds like fun actually."

Aidan nodded. "When do we start?"

"Let's go to the house and get them set up. I have extra memory cards for each of them too. We can change cards if there's something on them. My only problem is that I have to fly to Chicago tomorrow to meet my publisher. Can you guys get them out and start monitoring them?"

The boys nodded. "We'll take care of it don't worry."

Then Aidan added, "You know we have that camera set up already too, we haven't looked at it for a long time. We better check it out too."

"Mike do you have any extra memory cards other than for your cams?"

Mike nodded. "I'll give you one for your camera too. Bring the one that's in it up to the house when you get them out and we'll check it to see if he's been around. Boy I really hope he's not going out hunting away from the valley. If that happens were going to have a bunch of irate people looking to go cougar hunting."

"We sure don't want that. It won't take long and we'll have people cougar hunting," Aidan said.

"Let's go and get those cameras."

They all had worried looks on their faces as they hiked up to the house. If Spirit was ranging out of the valley it could mean nothing but trouble.

 **Chapter 20**

The boys loaded Mike's cameras into the truck and took them to Aidan's house. They put them into his room for the time being, planning on working on getting them set up on Saturday.

The rest of the week went quietly at school and Saturday morning they loaded up the 4 wheelers and headed to the valley. Since they had the box of cameras and they planned on staying overnight in their tent, they decided to leave Sally at home. She was very disappointed and Aidan felt pretty guilty when they pulled out of the yard. They were hoping to get a glimpse of the cat and it was much less likely if they had a dog galloping around the valley while they worked. Plus they weren't sure the cat might attack Sally if she happened to get too close and they didn't want that to happen, so poor old Sal got left behind.

They parked the vehicles by the tent and stood there looking up and down the valley. "So where first?" Aidan said.

"Let's take a couple up near where we have our cam," Dylan said. "Then we can check it and change the memory card and find some more places in that area for the others."

"I think that's a good idea. We should put one down by the creek where he fishes, and maybe one by the pond, and we'll just figure out the others," Aidan said.

They each carried one camera and hiked up to the place where their camera was strapped to the tree on the trail. Dylan opened the plastic case and removed the camera and replaced the memory card, then he put the camera back inside and they closed it up.

Aidan was ahead of him hiking up onto the top of the rocky cliffs so he found a trail that led down toward the valley from the cliffs. Half an hour later they were walking back down the valley toward the campsite. "I was thinking that maybe a camera near the entrance to the valley might be a good idea," Dylan said as they got to the box and each picked up a second camera.

Aidan nodded. "Yeah that's a good idea. If somebody comes back here messing around again we can get a picture of who it is and they're busted. I'll go and put one down there. You do the two by the creek and pond."

"Ok, I'll take the extra one along and look for a trail leading north out of the valley. It'd be a good idea to see if he's really leaving or not."

By the time they were finished it was getting close to noon so they built a fire in their fire pit and cooked some hot dogs and ate. After lunch they got their fishing poles out and took their lawn chairs over near where the stream ran into the pond and fished for a couple of hours.

"Dang, this cast itches," Dylan said reaching down into the cast and scratching.

"How much longer do you have to have it on?" Aidan asked.

"I hope not much longer. It's driving me crazy."

Aidan had a bite and was feeling his line when they heard a grunt.

"Listen," Dylan said quietly.

They both sat very still and soon it came again. "What the

heck?"

Suddenly Dylan whispered, "Look up on the hillside."

Aidan looked and soon he saw movement. It was a wild pig. Then he noticed movement to the right of the critter and there was another smaller one. "Holy smokes, a mama and a baby," he said.

"More than one baby," Dylan said pointing farther up the hill. Sure enough there were three more little pigs and then Dylan spotted another baby.

"Five babies," Dylan said.

They sat watching the mother pig sniffing and rooting in the leaves and the babies scampering around doing the same. They moved along the hillside getting closer to the boys as they foraged.

"Kinda cool," Dylan said grinning.

"Yeah, I wonder where they came from? We're not suppose to have wild pigs in Wisconsin."

"We're not supposed to have cougars either," Dylan said. "I heard a rumor that some guys north of here in the next county hauled some of them up here from Missouri or someplace like that. They'd gone hunting for them down there and thought it'd be fun to have some on their farm. Of course the wild pigs multiply like rabbits and soon they moved from that farm to another and now they're all over the place."

"Yeah I heard that too. We'll have them forever now. Once something like that gets started it's almost impossible to get rid of them," Aidan said.

Aidan's line suddenly started jerking and he set the hook into a nice trout. As he was reeling it in they were watching the pigs. Just as Aidan got the trout to shore Dylan gasped. "Look!"

Aidan looked up at the hillside just in time to see the cougar spring up from the back side of a brush pile. One second there was nothing there and the next second the cat was moving like lightning across the short distance between it and one of the piglets. The little pig didn't have a chance. Before it could even take a step the cat had it by the throat. The little pig squealed twice and went silent. The rest of the pigs went running off down the hill squealing and grunting all the way.

"Holy smokes," Aidan said holding his pole with the trout dangling from it.

The cat stood watching the pigs run off. The one he had caught hung limply in his mouth. He turned and started down the hill diagonally toward the boys. They sat still and watched as he got to the floor of the valley, walked up to the stream and jumped gracefully across with the pig in his jaws. When he got on the other side of the stream he stopped and looked right at the boys. He stood there staring at them, his tail twitching back and forth. Then he made a couple of long strides and loped up the hill on the other side of the valley toward the cliffs.

Aidan's heart was beating like a hammer. "Did you see that? He stood there like he was showing off his kill."

"Wow, that was amazing," Dylan said. "Just freaking amazing!"

 **Chapter 21**

The boys fished for a while longer and then fixed their supper over the fire. They'd brought some brats and potatoes so they sat a frying pan on their steel grate over the fire and fried the potatoes and then when they were just about done they put the brats on long forks and grilled them. They sat on their lawn chairs and ate and talked about the day.

"Seeing those wild pigs makes me even surer that our cougar wasn't the one who took that little dog," Dylan said.

"I've been thinking that too," Aidan answered. "Why would he travel all that way to eat a dog when he has turkeys and pigs right here, not to mention deer, rabbits and squirrels?"

"And trout when he wants one," Dylan added.

"Yeah, that too."

"Tomorrow we'll have to go up and talk to Mike and tell him what we found," Dylan said. "We'll see what he says, since he's the expert."

"I'm thinking it's not a cat at all," Aidan said, "maybe it's a coyote or a tan colored dog."

"That's possible, but how could you mistake a coyote for a cat?"

"You remember who saw it don't you?"

Dylan laughed. "Yeah, I guess Susie is kind of a bimbo after all."

They sat and talked and burned firewood until the air began to cool off and then crawled into their tent, took off their outer clothes and slid into their sleeping bags. "Do you suppose those trout are ok on the stringer?" Aidan asked.

"I'm not going to get up now and clean them," Dylan said.

Aidan laughed. "Me either, I guess they'll be ok."

It was several hours later when Aidan woke. He wasn't sure if he'd heard something but he knew he had to go to the bathroom. He turned over and tried to think of something else but it was no use, so he got up and slipped out of the tent into the chilly night. He was in his boxers and barefoot so he walked a reasonable distance from the tent and peed. He was shivering a bit and hurried as much as possible. When he turned to go back to the tent he stopped short.

Twenty feet from him, just on the back side of the tent, the cougar was lying in the grass watching him. "Holy crap!" he thought to himself. He stood perfectly still and looked at the cat. It was lying on the ground with its chin on its front paws, ears up, staring at him. The cat's tail twitched back and forth silently.

Aidan didn't know what to do. If the cat was going to attack he was in trouble. For one thing the cat would get to him before he got to the tent, and for a second thing the nylon tent wasn't going to stop the cat if he wanted to get Aidan and Dylan.

Suddenly he started shivering. He pulled his arms in next to his body to keep himself as warm as possible. The cat never moved, just looked at him.

"I've got to do something," Aidan thought.

He finally decided to move toward the tent. He took a small step and the cat's ears perked forward. Aidan stopped and then took another step. The cat just watched.

Finally Aidan got the courage to try moving to the tent. He took slow steps and the cat watched, the tip of its tail moving slowly back and forth. Aidan got to the tent and crouched down and crawled inside. He turned and zipped the flap closed as quickly as possible. Then he got into his sleeping bag and began to shake uncontrollably, partly from the cold and partly from the scare of the cat.

"Dylan," Aidan whispered. He shook his friend. "Dylan," he whispered again.

"What?" Dylan said sleepily.

"The cougar, it's right outside the tent."

Dylan sat up. "What did you say?"

"Shhh, I went out to pee and the cougar is crouched out there behind the tent about ten feet away, watching us."

"Are you sure? Maybe you had a dream."

Aidan punched Dylan in the arm. "It wasn't a dream, I had to pee and when I went out that cat was lying there watching our tent."

Dylan rubbed his shoulder. "Jeez, chill, I was just asking. Did he look like he was going to attack you?"

"Not really, he looked like he was just watching us. It was kind of crazy."

Dylan zipped open his sleeping bag. "I'm gonna look."

"Be careful, he's right out there behind us."

Dylan slowly zipped the door open trying not to make too much noise. He crawled out of the tent and Aidan heard him stand up. "Dylan... Dylan?"

"I'm here. I don't see anything but our lawn chairs."

"Is he gone?"

"If he was ever here he's gone now," Dylan said.

"What do you mean 'If he was here.'?

"I mean maybe the shadows looked like a cougar."

"You think I mistook a lawn chair for a cougar?"

"Well, maybe the shadows..." Dylan began to laugh.

Aidan jumped out of his sleeping bag and crawled out. "I'm not crazy. He was right there," he said pointing to an empty spot on the ground.

Dylan shrugged. Aidan walked over and put his hand on the grass. "Come here, feel this."

Dylan walked over and touched the ground. He looked up. "It's warm," he said. Then they heard a branch snap up on the hill toward the cliffs. "There!" Dylan said.

Even in the dark they could see the cougar moving off up the hill.

"What the heck is going on?" Aidan asked.

"Danged if I know. We need to talk to Mike."

 **Chapter 22**

Aidan lay awake in the tent feeling the warmth of the sun as it heated up the tent fabric, thinking about the strange way the cat had acted the previous night. "It almost seemed like he wanted to be friendly," he thought. "I don't think that's something that's ever happened before. I'll have to ask Mike, he'll know."

Dylan rolled over and opened his eyes. "Mornin," he said. "I'm hungry, how about a couple of trout for breakfast?"

Aidan grinned. "You forgot to clean them last night. Does that mean you're going to clean them now while I get the fire going?"

"You do such a good job on trout," Dylan said with a half smile, "why don't I get the fire going and peel some potatoes?"

"Oh yeah, you think flattery will get you out of the cleaning job? I'm not that dumb. But I really don't mind. I'll clean them but you get your lazy butt up and get the other stuff ready."

Dylan grinned like a fox as Aidan slid out of his sleeping bag and put on his shorts and tee shirt. The grass was still wet outside so he stayed barefoot. He walked off a way and did his morning business and then went down by the pond and picked up the stringer that was held down by a rock. The four trout were all still alive and flopping as he carried them up to the campsite. They had an old wooden crate that they used as a table and Aidan grabbed their chopping block and put it on top of the crate so he could clean the fish.

Dylan soon came from the tent and stirred the embers of their fire and had a good blaze going in no time. Then he went and dipped a kettle of water from the stream and washed the potatoes and began slicing them into a frying pan.

Aidan had two of the fish cleaned and was starting on the

third when he felt like he was being watched. He stopped and looked up slowly toward the woods. His eyes got big and he whispered to Dylan. "Dyl... the cats up there watching us."

Dylan looked at Aidan and then looked where he was looking. "Holy smokes," he said.

They watched as the cat climbed up on a flat rock and lay down watching the camp. His tail twitched back and forth very contentedly.

"He looks like he's just enjoying watching us," Aidan said quietly.

"Like a barn cat," Dylan added. "Give him a fish."

"What? You think he wants a handout?"

"I don't know. He likes fish, toss one up toward him and see what he does."

Aidan picked up one of the fish that hadn't been cleaned yet. He walked slowly over toward the cat. It watched him but didn't get up and run. When he got close enough he gave the fish a throw up toward the cat. When he did it the cat jumped to his feet and took a couple of steps backward. Then it stopped and looked at the fish flopping in the grass at the edge of the woods. He looked at the fish and then at the boys.

"Stay still... don't move," Aidan said.

The cat watched the trout flopping and moved forward toward it a couple of steps. He looked at the boys and then sprinted forward, grabbed the fish and ran back into the woods.

"Oh my gosh, that's amazing," Dylan said.

They could see the cat up in the woods as he held the fish between his front paws just like one of their barn cats would do, and began to eat it. When the fish was gone the cat looked down at the boys and licked its face.

"That's all you get, the rest are for us," Aidan said.

The cat walked down and lay on the flat rock again and seemed like it was going to take a nap.

"Would you look at that?" Dylan said. "The dang thing thinks it's a house cat."

Aidan just shook his head. "This is very strange Dylan."

They went back to their work and soon they were eating fried potatoes and trout. The cat lay dozing... occasionally looking up when a pan clanked or one of the boys said something a little louder than usual.

They finished up their breakfast, washed up the pan and dishes and put things away. They dipped some water from the stream for brushing their teeth and washing up and then decided to hike up the valley and up the hillside to Mike's house. "We'll get the extra storage chips and check the trail cameras. I guess we know that the cat lives here now, but we might get some cool pictures anyway," Aidan said as they walked along.

"If nothing else we can see where he spends most of his time," Dylan added.

When they got to the end of the valley they hiked up the trail that led to Mike's land and the hill point where they'd sat and first watched the cat fish from the stream. As they got to the top they found Mike sitting on the point watching them come up. "Morning," he said to them.

"Hey Mike, you won't believe what we've seen in the past day," Aidan said huffing from the steep climb.

"Oh I think I might believe you. I saw what happened this morning. I've been here since dawn. Did you know Spirit followed you up the valley?"

The boys looked down the hill. "He followed us?"

"He was up in the woods just above you all the way."

"Mike," Aidan said, "have you ever seen a cougar that acted like this?"

Mike shook his head. "This is something that I've never even heard of happening."

"What do you think he's up to?"

"Boys, I have no idea, no idea at all."

 Chapter 23

The three of them were sitting in Mike's living room around the fireplace. "There are cougars that were raised from kittens that have been used in circus acts, but as far as a cat from the wild having interest in humans, that's just something I've never heard of or read about," Mike said.

"You don't think maybe it's because he took our fish that first night or we gave him a fish yesterday?" Aidan asked.

"I doubt it. He's not hungry. He can catch a fish almost any time he wants one. He gets a turkey quite often, there are surely enough rabbits and squirrels for him to stay full most of the time and now I've been seeing wild pigs quite often, so I'd suppose that he's found them too."

"He did for sure," Dylan said. "We saw him catch one yesterday. It was a mama pig and a bunch of little ones and he got one of the little guys without much trouble at all."

"That's what I mean, he's not hungry. He seems to just be interested in watching what you guys do. It's like he's curious."

"You know what they say about curious cats," Aidan said.

Mike nodded. "Cats are naturally curious, and cougars are just big cats."

"Do you think we might be in danger?" Dylan asked.

"I'd be cautious. As long as you guys don't get to familiar with him, you'll probably be alright. Don't approach him. Let him make the move to you. And for sure don't corner him. You know, cougars are solitary animals. Out west where they normally live, they very seldom come across a human. This one has been alone for a long time looking for his own territory, and I think he's just getting used to seeing you guys out there and is curious."

"So we're probably not in any danger," Dylan said.

"I'd think you're ok. Actually with those wild pigs around I'd be more cautious about them. I haven't seen a boar yet but they can get pretty ornery. I've read about several times when a hunter or someone out in the woods just minding his own business was attacked by a big boar pig. They've got some nasty tusks and a nastier disposition, so I'd be careful about them. If the sows and little pigs are around, there surely is a boar or two around too."

"Should we keep a gun handy?"

"It wouldn't be a bad idea. I'd keep one at your camp for sure. If you're in the woods, you can climb a tree but out there on the flat ground, you'd be in trouble if one came after you. I don't think they'd just attack unless they felt threatened but they're kind of unpredictable."

"I've heard they can get really big," Dylan said.

"Oh that's for sure. I've heard of them weighing several hundred pounds. A pig like that could really injure you if not kill you. I don't know how they got to Wisconsin but they're going to change the ecology of the state. They multiply like... well like pigs. The sows have a litter every three months or so and they often have 8 or 10 piglets per litter. You can see how fast they could take over a patch of woods."

"We're going to check the cameras and change the memory cards. We'll keep our eyes open for those big boars," Aidan said.

"I'll get the extra ones," Mike said. "We'll number them so we know which camera they came from. The ones in the cameras all have numbers so replace them with the same number."

Mike got the memory cards and Dylan put them in his pocket. "Well, when you get them changed we can take a look and see what's lurking around out there," Mike said.

They walked out to the point and the boys started down the trail to the valley. Mike waved at them as they left. Then he sat down to watch.

The boys got to the first camera and opened it, changed out the memory card and snapped the housing shut. Then they hiked up the hill to the next and from there worked their way all along the hillside to the cliffs changing memory cards.

As they got to the camera closest to the cliffs and caves Dylan stopped and motioned to Aidan. He looked up the hill to a rocky point and there was Spirit looking over the edge, watching them. "Looks like our guardian angel is on duty," he said smiling.

"Dang, isn't that something? You think we're lucky much? How many other kids our age have a pet cougar?" Dylan said.

"I wouldn't call him a pet but he's sure an unusual critter."

They finished up and went down to their campsite. They picked up the site and put things away since they had school the next day. With everything stored in its place and the site all cleaned up they got on the 4 wheeler and headed out of the valley.

"Bye Spirit," Dylan said as they passed through the trail in the cut. "See you soon."

Chapter 24

"I called Mike during lunch and he said to come up after school so we could look at the cam pictures. He also said he'd grill some brats for us," Dylan said as he and Aidan walked out of school after the last bell.

"Cool, I'm anxious to see if we can figure out where Spirit lives."

They rode the school bus home and then Dylan returned with his dad's pickup half an hour later to pick up Aidan. They pulled into Mike's yard and could see smoke coming from the grill. Aidan grinned as they got out of the pickup. "Mmmm brats, the food of the gods," he said.

Mike came out and they talked while the brats finished cooking. Then they went inside and feasted on the brats and all the extras Mike had fixed. "Jeez, you're a good cook," Dylan said around a mouthful of brat.

"I like to cook especially when I have company. Otherwise it seems like a lot of work for only one person," Mike said.

"Were you ever married?" Dylan asked.

"No, I came close once but it seemed like school and jobs kept me kind of unsettled. I moved from place to place doing studies on one kind of critter or another and my fiancé decided she didn't want to be married to a gypsy, so it kind of fell through and so far I'm still looking."

"We used to think girls were yucky but lately they've been

looking better," Dylan said.

Mike laughed. "Yeah, I bet so. You guys have lots of time to find that right one. The problem many people have is that they get too intense too fast and in a couple of years they aren't as happy as they thought they'd be and it's over. I don't want that, I want someone forever or not at all."

The boys nodded. "You're probably the smartest guy around."

"So you brought the memory cards?"

Aidan went to his jacket and brought a plastic bag with the devices in it to the table. Mike got his laptop and powered it up. He put in chip #1 and they watched it load. Then he began to scroll through the pictures.

"Looks like there are five pictures," he said. "Hmm, there's a squirrel, a squirrel, two squirrels, an owl and whoa, an owl with a squirrel in his claws."

The boys laughed. "That's an unlucky squirrel for sure," Aidan said.

"Well the cat doesn't live around that camera I guess," Mike said.

They looked through the next memory card with much the same results. The only difference was that this one had a couple of turkeys on it and an opossum. When they got to the next one they finally saw Spirit.

"Ok, there he is. This one was just below the rock cliffs wasn't it?" Mike asked.

"Yeah, right on the deer trail that leads up to the rocks."

There were nine pictures and seven of them were of the cat coming or going. There was one picture of a turkey crossing the trail and one of a deer.

The next memory card was the one facing the rocks and cliffs from on top of the hillside. It had several pictures of the cat.

"Notice he's always close to that steep ledge?" Mike asked.

"Yeah, and I've been up there years ago and there's a cave

back in the hill from that ledge," Aidan said.

Mike nodded. "Then that's where he is staying. He might not sleep there every night but I'd bet he's on that ledge sleeping in good weather and in the cave when it's cold or raining. He can see the whole hillside from there and if something to eat comes along or some danger appears. He's up where he can attack or hide without much trouble."

"Kind of a perfect spot for him isn't it?" Dylan said.

"This is the exact thing a cougar would look for. There's a place to hide, lots of food, not much traffic from humans except for you guys, and he seems to be ok with sharing the valley with you."

They put the next card in and began scrolling through it. "Whoa, look at that!" Dylan said when they got to the fifth picture.

"That's one ugly pig," Aidan said.

The picture was of a wild boar looking right at the camera. You could see the bristles on his snout and his tusks, yellowed and curling up each side of his mouth.

"Jeez that thing is big," Dylan said. "That camera was about three feet off the ground and that thing is looking right at it."

"He looks big and probably is mean too," Mike said. "You guys need to be careful out there. A boar like this isn't afraid of much. He'll steer clear of the cat but if you get too close to him you never know if he'll run or attack. They're pretty nasty critters. I think you guys should carry a gun of some kind when you're in the valley until we see what this guy is like."

"My dad's got a 9mm pistol," Aidan said.

"That'd be good. If nothing else it makes a heck of a bang and would probably scare him away, and if not it'd stop him."

"I'll get it when we go home and from now on we'll carry it with us."

They looked at the last memory card and there were several pictures on it. The first five were squirrels and hen turkeys and the sixth one got their attention.

"Holy smokes look at that tom."

There was a tom turkey standing on the trail all fanned out displaying for several hens that they could see in the background. The next picture was the same turkey turned toward the camera.

"Look at that, he's got more than one beard," Aidan said.

Sure enough the bird had multiple beards.

"Look at those spurs, they're huge," Dylan said pointing to the screen.

"That's a trophy," Mike said.

Aidan turned toward them and smiled. "Guess who's turkey season starts next Wednesday?"

"You think you're good enough to fool him?" Mike asked.

"Knowing where they hang out is half the battle, I know where this guy lives, I'll be there and if he shows up, he'll be mine."

"Well, I guess we'll see, won't we?" Dylan said grinning.

Chapter 25

The boys gathered their food and drove the 4 wheeler to the valley Friday after school. The plan was to get up at dawn and listen to where the turkeys were when they started gobbling the next morning. That would give Aidan a better idea of where to put his blind when his turkey season started on Wednesday.

"So you think you'll get that big boy?" Dylan asked with a grin on his face.

"Do you doubt my hunting skills?" Aidan asked.

"Yup."

Aidan socked Dylan in the shoulder. "You'll think different when I bring that world record in," he said.

They got their camp set up and sat in their lawn chairs with a fire going just talking and looking at the valley. "Do you know how lucky we are to have a place like this?" Aidan asked.

"Yeah, I do, and I'm darn glad we have it."

Dylan got out their hot dogs and they cooked them on sticks over the fire and ate chips and cookies.

"I wonder if Spirit is up there watching us?" Dylan said.

"I'd bet on it," Aidan said.

Dusk was beginning to grow into dark when they heard the

gobble. They both looked up the valley toward where the sound had some from.

"That's pretty close to where the camera is," Dylan said.

Aidan nodded. "Tomorrow we'll listen and then later in the morning when he's out chasing hens we'll sneak up there and put up a blind. Then Wednesday I'll be there in the dark and he won't know what hit him."

Dylan grinned. "You hope."

"I'm getting cold, let's go to bed," Aidan said.

They let the fire burn down and one by one crawled into the tent. Aidan was last one in and he stopped and looked up the valley. He could feel the eyes of the cat watching him... and it was kind of comforting feeling.

Aidan's cell phone began beeping and he grabbed it and turned off the alarm.

"What time is it?" Dylan asked groggily.

"It's 4:30. The sun is up at a little after 6 but I want to be out there in the dark to get close to that big bird."

Dylan sighed. "Let's go," he said.

They dressed and put camouflage clothes on the top layer and hiked up the valley quietly by the light of the stars. When they got close to the area they thought the turkey roosted they walked up into the woods a little way and sat down beside two trees that were wide enough to hide their profiles.

"Now we wait," Dylan whispered.

When they'd been sitting about fifteen minutes they heard the sound of something shuffling past in the leaves. "Probably a coon or possum," Aidan thought to himself.

A few minutes later they heard a hen turkey yelp twice from the roost. Aidan looked over at Dylan and he nodded that he'd heard. A few minutes later a second hen yelped quietly answering the first.

The hens were down the hill a little way and to the north of where they were sitting. Normally hens and toms didn't roost together so he hoped the toms were near to where they were sitting.

In nature, the hens do a few roost yelps to let each other know where they are and when it gets light enough, they fly down to the ground and begin to feed on acorns, berries, leaves and almost anything else they can find.

The toms roost nearby and usually will gobble from the roost before they fly down. If they're close enough to the hens they sometimes will fly down and land right with the hens. If they're farther away they'll fly down and gobble and the hens will come to them to be bred. Once each hen is bred she goes off and lays an egg. When all the hens have been bred the toms go off in search of food and usually find a prominent place to stand and fluff their feathers up to display how beautiful they are to any other hens that might have not seen them yet.

Hunting turkeys turns the game around a bit. The hunter tries to get close to the tom's roost area and puts out a hen decoy or two and hides. Then he yelps like a hen that is looking for the tom but can't find him. Finally the tom gets impatient and goes looking for that "lost" hen and Boom, game over. At least that's the way it's intended to happen. The one thing that most turkey hunters find out quite quickly is that what they expect to happen often doesn't. The old adage of: "If something can go wrong... it will," happens more in turkey hunting than any other.

Soon hens began yelping and it sounded like there must be half a dozen or more roosting together. Then Aidan heard the rustle of one of them as she flew down to the ground.

Suddenly a tom gobbled just up the hill from them. Aidan turned his head very slowly and watched. The tom gobbled again and then a second one gobbled. The hens answered the gobbles. Next a tom flew down to the ground and it was about forty yards up the hill. Then a second flew down and a third followed. The big tom was one of the three and he was obviously the dominant bird. He puffed up and began strutting while the other two just stood off to the side. There is a definite pecking order in any group of turkeys, with a dominant tom and a dominant hen in each group.

"Holy smokes," Dylan whispered.

"He's a monster," Aidan replied.

The turkey was huge. Instead of a thin tassel of coarse hair hanging from his chest, this bird had a beard that looked like a horse tail. It was very thick and looked to be nearly a foot long. He strutted and drummed, and began working his way toward the hens. Suddenly he stretched his neck out and gobbled. Both of the boys jumped at how loud it was.

They watched mesmerized as the hens began arriving for their morning appointment with the boss tom. Aidan was absorbed watching the breeding spectacle when he heard Dylan whisper, "Aidan, look up on the hill."

Spirit was lying behind a blown down log watching.

Chapter 26

"Oh no, I hope he's not gonna try to catch that big tom turkey," Aidan whispered.

"He'll screw up your hunt for sure if he shows himself," Dylan whispered back.

The turkeys kept on with what they were doing, moving steadily down the hill toward the valley. As the big tom bred each hen she scurried off to wherever her nest was located to lay her egg of the day. Each hen had a different goal but they all laid one egg a day until they got what they considered the right amount of eggs and then they began sitting on them. By a miracle of nature, all of the eggs hatched at the same time once they were incubated properly.

The boys watched and the cat stayed put as the turkeys moved on down the hillside. Eventually all the hens were gone and the three toms worked their way out into the open sunshine. The big one began to display. The other two would get their feathers about half way up and then would chicken out if the big guy looked their way. He was the boss and until he met his end the other two waited their turn.

"Thank God that cougar didn't go after the turkeys," Aidan finally said.

He looked up the hill but couldn't see the cat. "It looks like he left," he said.

"Yeah, I saw him slink up over the hill when the toms left. What do you suppose he was doing? Do you think he was after a turkey or just watching us?"

"Jeez, I don't know. It's kind of spooky thinking that he's watching us isn't it?

Dylan nodded. "I'm not afraid of him it just seems strange

he'd be so interested in us."

"Well, let's hike back to camp and have breakfast. Then we can come back up and get that blind built. Those toms will be out all day so we don't have to worry about seeing them back up here until dusk."

They walked back to camp and built up the fire and made breakfast. A short while later they were eating bacon and eggs sitting in their lawn chairs. "Boy that's a big turkey," Aidan said.

"I've never seen one with a beard that thick. It has to have several beards. And his spurs are huge, I wonder if he'll be a record breaker?"

"I haven't got him yet," Aidan said.

"Well if you don't get him, I will. I have next season you know."

"We'll see, don't clear a place on your wall for a mount just yet," Aidan laughed.

"Do you know how to measure a tom to see what he scores?" Dylan asked.

"Yeah, you weigh them and they count one point for each pound and partial points for ounces. Then you measure their beard and take that times two. With a multiple beard bird you measure them all. Then you measure the spur and take that times ten. It's kind of complicated but that's the way they do it for the record book. That big guy will score a lot of points. He'd be a real trophy."

They cleaned up from breakfast and picked up a roll of camouflage material and a staple gun from the 4 wheeler. Then they hiked up the hill and chose a spot between where the hens roosted and where the toms roosted.

"If everything is the same they'll roost here," Aidan said. "If it happens to be windy they might change but if that happens I'll have to wing it and not use the blind."

"A blind makes it nice but I've gotten a couple birds without one," Dylan said.

"Yeah, me too but as long as we are here we might as well

make one."

They cleared out an area of leaves and sticks and then chose several small saplings and chopped them off with Dylan's machete. They stuck them into the ground and stapled the camouflage cloth to them creating a little hide that they could sit behind. After the blind was built they stuck extra sticks and weeds into the ground around it to make it blend in better and stood back to check it out.

"It looks good," Aidan said.

"Yup, should work like a charm. All you have to worry about is if Sprit decides to come and sit with you."

Aidan grinned. "Don't say that."

They went back to the camp and fished for a couple of hours, catching 6 nice trout. Aidan volunteered to clean them while Dylan did the rest of the chores for supper. Aidan left one trout on the stringer in the water.

After they ate supper they sat by the fire talking. The stars were out and the moon was nearly full, casting a bluish light over the valley. "I'm getting my cast off tomorrow after school," Dylan said.

"No kidding? That's good you're kind of clumsy with it on. Do you..."

"Do I what?"

Aidan nodded toward the south. Dylan turned and looked. Spirit was lying on the ground about twenty feet from them, looking at them.

"Wow, he's sure quiet."

"I left a fish on the stringer. I'm going to get it for him," Aidan said.

Dylan grinned.

Aidan got up slowly. The cat raised his head but didn't move away. Aidan walked over to the bank and pulled the stringer up out of the water. The cat saw the fish flopping on the stringer and his ears perked forward. Aidan took the fish off the stringer and turned toward the cat. "Here boy, we saved a fish for you," he said quietly.

He took a couple of slow steps toward the cat. It tensed but didn't move. He took a few more steps and held out the fish. The cat got to his feet and took two steps toward Aidan.

"Holy crap" Dylan whispered.

Aidan held the fish out and crouched down. The cat moved closer and then stopped. "Not sure yet? Ok, this is ok," Aidan said.

He tossed the fish to the cat and it landed at his feet. The trout began to flop around and the cat put one of his front paws on it. He looked at Aidan and then at Dylan and reached down and picked up the fish in his jaws.

"Good boy," Aidan said.

The cat whirled around and loped off down the valley toward the cliffs. When he got about fifty yards away he stopped, turned and looked back. Then he went off into the woods.

"Are you kidding me?" Dylan said.

Aidan let his breath out. "If you'd have told me you did that I wouldn't have believed you."

"This is way cool," Dylan said shaking his head. "Way cool."

Chapter 27

The boys sat around for a while and then loaded up and left for home. Dylan didn't ride the bus in the morning since he had to get his cast cut off, so Aidan was looking forward to seeing him at school. During the noon lunch break Dylan came into the cafeteria grinning and holding up his arm, which was cast free.

"All better," he said sitting down at Aidan and some of their other friend's table.

"Does it hurt at all?" Aidan asked.

"Nope, it kind of feels funny without the cast but I'm glad to get rid of it. I should have saved it and brought it back and hit Clifford over the head with it."

On Tuesday Aidan packed up his hunting clothes and some food and left for the valley. Dylan had chores to do so Aidan decided to camp in the valley by himself so he'd be right there in the morning for his turkey hunt. He got to the valley and opened up the camp. He built a fire and settled back to enjoy the evening. He'd brought a package of hot dogs and buns along and was kind of roughing as far as food was concerned. He cut a hot dog stick and roasted three of them one after the other and ate as he roasted. When he was done he sat back and looked into the fire while the daylight slowly turned deeper and deeper blue until it was black.

It seemed kind of strange to be there alone. It was unusual for him to be on his own since Dylan and he did everything together. He went into the tent and got a sweatshirt and put it on and when he came back out Spirit was lying a few yards away on the grass.

"Hello boy," Aidan said quietly. "I don't have any fish for you tonight, sorry."

The cat looked at him and twitched his tail.

"Hey how about a hot dog?"

Aidan reached over and opened his cooler and took a wiener out. He held it up so the cat could see it and then he tossed it toward him. The wiener landed a few feet short and Spirit leaned forward sniffing. He looked at Aidan and then got up and took a couple steps forward and snatched up the wiener, backed up and lay down with it in his mouth. He dropped it on the ground, smelled it, and gulped it down.

"Hey, good huh?" Aidan said. "Want another one?"

Aidan got another wiener and this time he tossed shorter than before. The cat got up and didn't hesitate and came right up and picked up the wiener and ate it. Then he stood there twitching his tail looking at Aidan.

"You like those hey? I've got three more, want them?"

He opened the cooler and one by one he fed the wieners to the cat. When he got to the last one he held it out in his hand toward the cat. Spirit looked at him and then at the wiener. "You gotta take this one from my hand," Aidan said quietly.

The cat moved forward and stretched his neck out and nibbled the wiener from his hand and gulped it down.

Aidan's hand was shaking but he was grinning as wide as the sky above. "Good boy Spirit, good boy," he said.

The cat stood there for a minute and then turned and walked slowly away from the camp. "See you tomorrow," Aidan said.

As he lay in the dark tent alone Aidan had to marvel at what had happened. "Jeez, Dylan won't believe me," he said to himself. "Amazing, just freaking amazing."

Aidan woke with a start when his cell phone alarm went off at 5 am. He yawned and stretched and lay there in his warm sleeping bag dreading getting out to dress. Finally he jumped out and put on his cold clothes as fast as he could. He went outside and did his morning duties and got his turkey hunting gear together. He was wearing full camouflage including a head net and gloves. He had his 12 gauge turkey gun loaded with 3 ½ inch #4 magnum turkey loads and a hen decoy that folded up to fit in his pocket. He checked to see if his diaphragm turkey call was in his upper pocket and it was where it should be.

"Well, I think I've got everything," he thought to himself.

He started down the valley staying out in the open until he got to about where he thought he should start up the hill to his turkey blind. He went slowly because just south of him the hens should be roosting and just a little north and up the hill from him, the toms hopefully were roosting. He wanted to get into his blind without spooking either of the groups.

There was enough light from the stars that he could see fairly well. He took it very slow and careful so he wouldn't step on a branch or roll a rock down the hill. About halfway up the hill he stopped and looked and saw his blind up ahead. He was right on track.

When he got to the blind he unhooked one corner of the camouflage material and stepped inside the little enclosure. He re-hooked the camo and sat down with his back against the tree. He was facing downhill overlooking the game trail that the toms had followed earlier when he and Dylan had scouted them. If all went well they'd pass from his left and go right in front of his blind where he'd make that big one Thanksgiving dinner.

He pulled his facemask down over his face, got his turkey call from his pocket and laid the gun across his lap. "Now all I have to do is wait," he thought.

After several minutes the sounds of the woods began again after he'd disturbed the little critters of the dark by walking in on them. There were sounds of little feet scurrying through the leaves and chirps from mice and voles. Soon one of the early waking birds began to chirp. The sky was beginning to turn from black to deep blue. The day was beginning.

In the next fifteen minutes more birds began to sing, a squirrel barked and an opossum shuffled past on the game trail. Down in the valley he heard a hen mallard quacking and somewhere above in the still dark sky a flock of geese passed over, honking.

Below him a robin began to sing its early morning song. The bird sang and sang and Aidan smiled as he listened to it. "She's happy this morning," he thought.

"It shouldn't be long now," he said quietly to himself. And just as the thought entered his mind, a hen turkey yelped from her roost below him in a tree.

 **Chapter 28**

A few minutes after the first hen yelped, another made a soft yelp from a tree to the right of the first one. Almost immediately after that the first hen yelped again followed by two more soft yelps from nearby trees.

"I'm right where I should be," Aidan thought to himself.

The hens began talking back and forth and soon the first gobble sounded from up on the hill to the left and behind Aidan. The gobble had hardly died away and two more came almost immediately. The first tom gobbled again, much deeper and bolder than the other two. Then he gobbled twice in a row.

"Oh man, he's here," Aidan thought. "And he's hot to trot."

Time seemed to move slowly. The minutes slipped past and eventually he heard the hens begin to fly down from the trees. They began to peep and cluck contentedly as they fed through the brush. Shortly afterward he heard the sound of the three toms as they flew to the ground.

Aidan was sitting with his knees up and the gun resting across his lap. He needed to get his gun up into position to shoot. From past experience that went very badly, he knew that if you tried to raise your gun when a turkey was in sight of you, they'd see the movement and the hunt would be over.

He just started to raise the gun when he saw the first hen starting down the trail.

"Oh no, I waited too long," he said to himself. "Well, I'll have to wait and see what happens."

The hen came past him and had no idea he was sitting ten yards from the trail in the blind. Soon a second hen came past and then two more came, picking and scratching. They were peeping and purring, sounds that meant "all is well" to turkeys. Aidan heard the big tom drumming from his left. Turkeys puff all up and raise their feathers so they look huge. They put their wings out to the sides and make a sound in their chest that sounds like a "boom" to impress the hens. This guy was drumming like crazy. Aidan turned his head about an inch and could see the tom mounting one of the hens.

"Dang, I should have been sitting on the upper side of the tree," he thought. He was in a position where he couldn't turn far enough to the left to shoot without moving his whole body, and if he tried that one of the hens or the toms would see him and the game would be over quickly. Turkeys have amazing eyesight and there were far too many turkey eyes looking around in the area for him to try to move. He'd get caught for sure.

The tom finished breeding the hen and another took her place. This went on for several minutes and the hens, one by one ran off to their nests to lay their egg.

"Well, hopefully when he's done he'll come down the trail," Aidan thought.

But it was not to be. When the last hen ran off the tom stuck his neck out and gobbled loudly. He stood there and fanned out again and waited. Then he gobbled again and the other two toms gobbled also.

"I could try to move and get a shot, or I can just sit still and not spook them and come back tomorrow," Aidan said inside his head. He decided if the toms didn't come down the path, he'd wait.

A few minutes later his mind was made up for him. A hen yelped off to the left down on the hill below them and the toms began waddling off toward her. Aidan watched his trophy get farther away and was pretty disappointed.

"Dang, I blew that," he said quietly to himself.

When the toms were out of sight he got up and stretched. He checked the time and it was time for him to get back to the house. He'd made arrangements to miss first hour at school and had about 45 minutes to get home, shower and get to class.

"Well, tomorrow is another day," he said and started down

the hill toward his camp.

Dylan was waiting by his locker when Aidan came walking down the hall just before second hour class was to start.

"Well?" he said.

"I messed up. I was right where I should have been but I was sitting too far to the right of the tree. I couldn't get my gun up far enough. Tomorrow I'm going to sit on the uphill side of the tree and I'll have his butt."

Dylan grinned. "Maybe you need me to go with you and give you a few pointers."

"As much as I hate to admit it, I missed having you there last night," Aidan said.

Dylan grinned. "Aw shucks, you missed me?"

"Not THAT much. Oh by the way, you missed something amazing."

"Spirit again?"

Aidan nodded just as the bell rang. "I fed him a hot dog and he took it from my fingers."

Dylan was still standing there with his mouth hanging open as Aidan walked into his class.

 **Chapter 29**

"And he took it out of your hand?"

Aidan nodded. "I tossed the first ones to him and kept getting them closer until I only had one left. Then I held it out and he just stretched his neck out and took it."

Dylan shook his head. "How many people have ever done that before? I'd bet no one."

"Are you coming tonight? I'm sure he'll show up. He thinks I'm his meal ticket now."

"You'd have to shoot me to keep me away," Dylan said.

They were sitting in the cafeteria at lunch apart from the other kids so their talk of the cougar wouldn't be heard.

"Well, we gotta make sure we have some extra food for him tonight too," Dylan said. "I gotta try that."

They arrived at the camp about an hour after school let out and put things in order. Since they had a couple of hours of daylight they decided to fish for a while. They were sitting talking and not catching much when Aidan noticed some movement on the hill above them. He looked carefully and saw Spirit stalking through the brush.

"Look he's up there trying to catch something," he said.

They looked up the hill and soon Dylan pointed. "It's one of those pigs, one of the little ones," he said.

They watched as the piglet rooted and scratched and as Spirit snuck closer and closer to the unsuspecting pig. He was getting close enough where he'd soon rush forward to attack when there came a snorting and squealing from above them. The mother pig must have seen Spirit. Suddenly there were pigs running all over the place. Spirit pounced forward but the little pig was moving fast up the hill. Spirit sprinted after if for a little way and then turned toward a different one that was going past. He missed it too and by the time he realized he wasn't going to catch it, all of the pigs were long gone.

"He missed," Dylan said laughing.

"Poor Spirit. I bet if he could talk he'd be cussing right now."

The cat stood there, his tail whipping back and forth.

Aidan whistled and the cat turned and looked down the hill at them. Aidan went to the cooler and got a wiener. He held it up.

"Holy smokes, he's coming," Dylan said.

Spirit came down the hill, jumped across the stream and walked up and lay down a little way from the boys.

"You had some bad luck up there," Aidan said to him. "How about a wiener?"

Aidan tossed a wiener to the cat and he gobbled it up.

"Amazing," Dylan said. "I'm going to try."

Dylan took a wiener from the cooler and held it out. The cat looked at him and then at Aidan. "It's ok," Aidan said.

Spirit got up and walked slowly forward. He stopped about three feet from the boys and Dylan reached out his hand with the wiener in his fingers. His hand was shaking like an old man with Parkinson's Disease.

Spirit took the wiener from his fingers and walked back, lay down and gulped it down.

"Well, believe me now?" Aidan asked.

"I'll never forget that as long as I live," Dylan said grinning from ear to ear.

"We're in unexplored territory my friend," Aidan said.

"No doubt."

They put away their fishing gear and got the fire going so they could roast their hot dogs. Spirit lay on the grass watching them like a house cat would. They ate hot dogs and fed Spirit the extras. When they were all gone he seemed to understand and got up and started up the valley toward his cave.

"See ya later boy," Aidan said.

They put things away and crawled into their tent. They undressed and got into their sleeping bags. Aidan set his alarm and then settled down.

"We gotta talk to Mike about this," Dylan said. "He'll think we're full of crap I bet."

"He's gone right now. I tried to call him but I remember he said a while back he had to go to New York for a book thing. I left a voice mail so hopefully he'll call."

"I can't wait to tell him, he'll poop," Dylan said laughing.

It seemed like they'd just lain down when the alarm went off. Dylan was moaning and groaning about why turkeys had to get up so early but Aidan ignored him and dressed and crawled out of the tent. He was checking his gun to be sure it was loaded when Dylan came out, dressed and ready to go.

"Let's go get a trophy," he said quietly.

They hiked up the valley and then up the same path that Aidan had taken the previous day. When they got to the blind Dylan sat on the downhill side and Aidan sat on the upper side where he'd be ready for the tom.

"I'm not screwing up today... as soon as I hear them gobbling I'm getting the gun up and ready."

"Good idea," Dylan whispered.

The morning came as before, with little squeaks and chirps and suddenly there were turkeys talking all around them. The hens began to yelp and right on cue the toms began to gobble from the tree. Soon the boys heard them all fly down.

"Not long now," Aidan whispered.

Soon the hens began to show up below them on the trail. Aidan had the gun up and ready to shoot. All he had to do was take off the safety.

One hen was even with the blind and two more were right behind it when the first one's head came up and she made a "Put!"

"Uh oh," Dylan whispered.

When a turkey hears one of his pals "Put" it puts everyone on alert. Heads come up and eyes look for danger. The whole group is alert looking for what is wrong and once it's seen, they are all leaving as quickly as possible.

The other two birds began to put and soon turkeys were scattering every which way, all away from the boys.

"What the heck?" Aidan said quietly.

"They didn't see us," Dylan said, "they were looking up behind us."

They heard the first grunt then. It was deep and throaty. Dylan looked at Aidan. He looked scared.

"Suppose that's that big boar?"

"Dang, I hope not."

The grunts began loudly, deep and dangerous sounding. Then the pig began squealing. His grunts grew louder and more angry sounding as he came down the hill getting closer and closer to them. They turned and saw the big boar they'd seen on the game camera and he was headed right at them.

"Run Dyl, go for a tree!"

They jumped to their feet. They had to jump over the low cloth blind. Aidan leapt over it and as soon as he'd cleared it he took off down the hill. Dylan caught his foot in the material and fell down but got up like a sprinter and began running down the hill. The boar was right behind him screaming and squealing.

"Hurry Aidan, get up a tree!" Dylan yelled from the lower branches of a medium sized maple. He had his hands free and was able to get up the tree fast after jumping several feet up when he got near it.

Aidan looked from right to left looking for a tree he could climb. The pig was getting closer. He had the shotgun in his hand but hadn't thought about shooting the pig. The gun though, made it hard for him to find a tree he could climb while holding it.

"Aidan, hurry."

Aidan could hear the pig right behind him and thought it was over when suddenly the pig's squealing changed from anger to fear. The angry grunts turned to high pitched screams. Aidan looked over his shoulder just as Spirit slammed into the pig. The two animals rolled down the hillside, over and over each other, with leaves and sticks flying.

 **Chapter 30**

Aidan found a tree he could climb and made it up far enough to feel safe from the angry pig. He was still clutching his 12 gauge in his hand. He looked down the hill and the pig and Spirit were both getting to their feet facing each other. Spirit made a charge and grabbed the pig by the back of the neck. The two animals began rolling around on the hillside, the pig squealing like crazy. The pig was huge... weighing in probably over 200 pounds and Spirit couldn't keep it from getting to its feet. The pig slammed his head back and forth and his tusk sunk into Spirit's shoulder. The cat screamed and let loose of the pig's neck. The pig charged and slammed his head into Spirit's side again and threw him several feet where he flew into the side of a large tree and fell to the ground stunned.

'Aidan, shoot that damn pig!" Dylan yelled. "He's gonna kill the cougar."

The pig was only fifteen feet from Aidan and was turning to charge into the cat. He raised the shotgun and put the bead on the pig's shoulder and pulled the trigger. The gun roared and the 3 ½ inches of #4 lead shot slammed into the pig's chest and tore a hole the size of a golf ball right through him. He dropped in his tracks.

Spirit lay stunned on the ground. He slowly got to his feet and stood looking at the pig and then at Aidan. There was blood running from his shoulder.

"Spirit, oh man, come on boy, let us help you," Aidan said.

The cat turned and loped up the hill toward the cliffs, limping badly on his right side.

"Oh man, Dylan, he's hurt bad," Aidan said.

Dylan climbed down from the tree he was in. "He saved us, he went after that pig because it was after us, you know."

"I'm sure of it," Aidan said. "But he needs medical help. He's bleeding badly and... Dylan what are we gonna do?"

"We gotta get hold of Mike, that's what we need to do," Dylan said.

"You're right. Let's go up to his place and see if he's back."

They left the pig lying where it had fallen and hiked down the hill and across the valley. They got to the trail that led up to Mike's place and hurried up the hill as fast as they could go.

"What if he's not home?" Aidan said, breathing hard from the fast climb.

"We'll worry about that when the time comes," Dylan answered.

They got to the point and followed it up to the house. Mike's vehicle was not there.

"Now what?"

"See if you have a cell signal," Dylan said.

Aidan opened his phone and nodded. "Yeah, I have one and I've got a voice mail."

He punched in his code and listened. "It's from Mike. He left it last night but I didn't have a signal down in the valley. He said he'll be home today around noon."

"What time is it now?"

"It's only a little past 6 am."

"Try calling him."

Aidan punched Mike's number into the phone and listened. It rang and rang. He looked up and shook his head. Then he got excited. "Mike? Mike, it's Aidan," he said.

"Mike I'm sorry to bother you so early but we've got a problem."

"Yeah, thanks, you know Spirit, well he's hurt and well it's a long story but he's hurt bad and we don't know what to do."

He listened. "Yeah, but Mike, he'll come right to us."

"Yeah... I'm sure... we've been feeding him hot dogs. No shit. Yeah, I'm not kidding."

He listened again. "Ok we're at your place. Ok, ok, all right, ok."

He closed the phone. "He's going to see if he can get an earlier flight. He might be here sooner but he'll be here by a little after noon at the latest."

"What did he say about Spirit?"

"He thinks we're crazy," Aidan laughed. "I don't think he believes me but I probably wouldn't believe me either. Anyway he told me where a key is and that there's some stuff in his house we can get ready so we can go and help Spirit when he gets here."

"We better call our parents and tell them to call the school," Dylan said.

"Oh yeah, man what are we gonna tell them?"

"Well we sure can't say our pet cougar got injured fighting a wild boar to keep his hot dog buddies safe. They'd think we're on drugs for sure."

"Wow, you're right about that."

"Well, let's just tell them we were turkey hunting and we have a wounded one out there we have to search for. That's close to what's going on."

"Dylan, you're a born liar, but... I like it."

Aidan called his mom and told her the story and she promised to call Dylan's parents and the school. The principal at the school was a turkey hunter so they knew he'd give them a little leeway when it came to hunting. They were both good students so it shouldn't be a problem.

"Well, now we wait," Dylan said.

 **Chapter 31**

They found the key where Mike said it would be and went into the house. Aidan checked to be sure the shotgun was on safe and stood it in the corner. They took off their jackets and boots.

"Mike said to make ourselves at home," Aidan said.

"I'm starved," Dylan replied, "I wonder what's in the fridge?"

Dylan opened the refrigerator and smiled. "Breakfast will be ready in about fifteen minutes."

Aidan nodded and went to the hallway and opened the second door on the left. It was a spare bedroom and Mike had told him there were some cases with animal tranquilizers in them as well as antibiotics and other drugs in a small refrigerator. Aidan carried the cases to the living room but left the refrigerated stuff alone for now. Then he found a case with some medical instruments and added that to his pile of gear.

"Come and get it," Dylan said from the kitchen.

Aidan walked in and smiled at the spread of food.

"We have bacon, eggs, toast and coffee," Dylan said grinning.

"You'd make somebody a good wife," Aidan said sitting down at the table.

They ate like they were starved Vikings and emptied all the platters. When they were done Dylan washed up the dishes and pans while Aidan went to the living room to open up the cases so Mike could find the things he needed for Spirit.

Dylan came into the living room and looked the gear over. "Jeez Mike must be pretty smart to know all about all this stuff and all the things he knows about so many things. No wonder he's a Doctor of lots of stuff."

"I suppose he uses this stuff if he's doing some study where they have to tranquilize animals to study them or track them," Aidan said.

"Well, all we can do now is get comfortable and wait," Dylan said. "It's nearly 10 o'clock hopefully he's on his way right now."

They sat down, Dylan in a recliner and Aidan on the couch. Dylan pulled the lever and put the recliner in "recline" position and Aidan stretched out and in no time they were both sleeping.

"Did I miss breakfast?"

Aidan opened his eyes. "Mike! Wow we must have fallen asleep. Am I ever glad to see you!"

Dylan opened his eyes and yawned. "You got here an hour early, that's good."

"I managed to get an earlier flight," Mike said. "So what's going on here? I'm not sure I heard what you said right."

Aidan began telling Mike about how the cat kept visiting them and how they fed it a fish and then about him feeding it hot dogs.

"And you actually held a hot dog in your hand it he took it from you?" Mike asked.

Aidan nodded. "It's like he's accepted us as part of his world."

"I've never heard of anything even close to this happening. I've seen cougars that were raised from babies that were in circus acts but never one from the wild that went out of his way to become friends with a person."

"He actually saved us from that big boar we saw on the trail cams," Dylan said.

"He must have been watching us hunt turkeys and when the pig started after us, he came in and took it down."

Mike shook his head. "That's amazing. So how bad do you think he's hurt?"

"The pig's tusk stuck him in the shoulder and then it slammed him with his big head. I know he's cut on the shoulder and maybe he's got broken ribs, I don't know. He was hurting, I'm sure of that," Aidan said.

"Well, we need to see if we can get close to him to take a look and see what's going on," Mike said. "I'm sure he'll hold up in his cave, but I don't know how close we can get. If we get too close he might feel trapped and attack us."

"I don't think he will," Aidan said.

"Aidan you can't be sure," Mike said, "this is a wild animal capable of killing you in less than a minute. This isn't a pet. He's a very dangerous wild critter."

"Well, I'm willing to take the chance," Aidan said.

"Me too," Dylan said. "We can't just let him get infection and die."

"You're right, of course. I'll get my dart gun and fill a tranquilizer dart. If we can get close enough I'm sure I can put a dart in him. Then we can clean his wound and give him a load of antibiotics."

"Do you have to shoot him?" Aidan asked. "What if he takes off and falls off the cliffs or something?"

"We have to sedate him, that's the only thing we can do," Mike said.

"I think we can do it another way," Aidan said.

Mike looked at them. "Another way? There is no other way."

Dylan grinned. "Mike do you have any sedatives in pill form?"

"Sure, why?"

"Got any hot dogs?"

Mike grinned. "No but I've got a bunch of rings of venison bologna in the freezer."

"Fire up the microwave," Aidan said.

 **Chapter 32**

Mike went to the freezer and got two rings of the venison bologna and thawed them out.

"It might even work better, it's thicker and we can make a little hole in it and hide a pill inside it. I'm sure he'll be fine with bologna," Aidan said.

They got things ready for the hike up to the caves. Aidan cut a ring of bologna up into two inch pieces and hid a sedative pill in three of them. Mike estimated the cat's weight at about a hundred and fifty pounds so he thought two pills should do the trick... if they could get Spirit to eat them. If not he prepared two darts that he could shoot into the cat to put him to sleep. Dylan filled a canteen with water and grabbed a pie pan so they could give him something to drink. The way he was limping as he ran away after his encounter with the pig, the boys figured Spirit wouldn't want to have to walk all the way to the valley floor for a drink, so they took him some water as well as the food.

When they were ready they packed everything into two backpacks and began the hike down the trail and then up the other side of the valley to the cliffs where they hoped to find the cougar.

"We were right up there," Aidan said pointing. "See, there's the pig lying in the leaves."

"Man, that's a big boar," Mike said. "Spirit was pretty brave going after that thing. It probably outweighs him by fifty pounds."

They stopped by the pig and looked down at the huge thing.

"Whew it stinks," Dylan said.

"It's a pig," Aidan said grinning.

They started up toward the cliffs where they last saw Spirit as he ran off. They went slowly and quietly so they wouldn't spook the cat. When they got beneath the cliffs they stopped and Mike began scanning with his binoculars. He looked back and forth across the area and then stopped and focused.

"There he is," he said pointing. "He's on that ledge up by that big pine tree. It looks like he's sleeping."

"Give me the bologna and let me go up," Aidan said. "He's most used to me and I think he'll trust me. If we all go up he might get spooked and run off."

The other two agreed. Aidan took the bag with the chunks of bologna in it. The three with pills inside them were clearly marked with a slit where they'd inserted the pills.

"Aidan wait," Mike said.

He handed Aidan a large heavy pistol. "Put this in your pocket."

"Mike he's not gonna hurt me," Aidan said.

"Yeah, probably not but just in case. He's injured, probably in a lot of pain and confused. You need this... just in case."

Aidan took the gun and put it in his jacket pocket and started climbing up the hill. As he got up nearly level with the cat he could see it had its eyes closed and was sleeping.

"We're going to get up on the hill a little higher and I'm going to get sighted in on him with the dart gun. If he acts like he's not going to let you close, just leave him alone and back off and I'll dart him," Mike said.

"Ok, but I think I'll be alright."

Aidan moved up the hill a little farther. 'It might be a good idea to let him know I'm here rather than just show up right in front of him when he wakes," he said to himself.

He made some noise by kicking a rock down the hill. The cat woke and looked up. It surveyed the area and then locked its eyes on Aidan. The tip of his tail began to flip back and forth. Aidan smiled, "Hey boy," he said. "Look what I've got for you."

Spirit watched Aidan climb up to the ledge and his tail

whipped back and forth more excitedly. He was glad to see his friend.

Aidan got down on his knees and crawled forward. "Are you hungry boy?" he said. He took one of the pieces of bologna that was not carrying a pill and put it out to the cat. Spirit sniffed it and gulped it from his hand. Aidan smiled. "Good huh? Want some more?"

Aidan fed the cat two of the chunks with sedatives inside them and then gave him two more regular pieces. All he had left was the one last one with a sedative. "We'll wait a bit for this one," he said.

The cat laid his head on his paws and looked up at Aidan.

"You were pretty brave going after that big old pig," Aidan said quietly to him. "You're a pretty brave boy."

The cat began to purr like a barn cat only much deeper. Aidan grinned. "Getting a little sleepy? Go ahead, I'll stay and keep you company."

The cat turned on his side and Aidan could see the jagged gash in his shoulder. It was crusted with dried blood and dirt. He looked back down at the cat and his eyes were closed. He was purring quietly, dead to the world.

Aidan looked down the hill and waved to Mike and Dylan to come up. The two of them climbed up and came out on the ledge.

"If I hadn't seen that with my own eyes I'd have never believed it," Mike said. "That's got to be a first, got to be."

"Just call me the cougar whisperer," Aidan said grinning.

 **Chapter 33**

Mike got right to work and opened his backpack to get his medicines and tools out. He took a sponge and poured some clean water on it and cleaned the wound. Then he cleaned it again with alcohol and put some salve on it.

"This is a topical antibiotic. It tastes pretty bad so I hope he won't lick it all off. Just in case he does, I'm going to give him a shot of antibiotic that should kill off the bacteria that got into him from that pig."

He filled a needle, pinched up the cat's skin and injected it under the skin.

"He's a beautiful animal isn't he," Mike said looking the sleeping cat over. "He looks to be pretty young." Mike lifted Spirit's lip and exposed his teeth. "Good clean new looking teeth. He's not very old, just like I suspected."

"You think this will fix him up?" Dylan asked.

"We'll have to watch him. If that gash heals, he'll be fine. It the gash gets nasty looking we might have to sedate him again or maybe Aidan can feed him antibiotics hidden in bologna. We'll wait and see," Mike said.

"This is a very rare opportunity," he added. "I doubt there have been half a dozen instances of being able to examine a wild cougar like this. I'm going to take some blood samples and then put a little tracking device under his skin. It's about the size of a quarter and will send out signals for six months to a year. I have a tracker at the house that will pick it up within a mile or so. We can keep track of him at least for a while."

Aidan sat down by the cat's head. "Can I touch him?" he asked.

"Sure, he's sleeping. He'll be under for another twenty minutes or so. Go ahead."

Aidan put his hand on the cat's head and stroked it like he would a barn cat. He ran his hand over the cat's shoulder and down its front leg.

"Jeez, it's all muscle," he said.

"They're amazingly strong and agile," Mike said. "Look at those back legs. These things can jump vertically five or six feet up in the air. They're a magnificent critter."

Dylan picked up one of Spirit's feet. He pressed on the pads and the claws came out. They were an inch and a half long and sharp as needles.

"Wow, look at those claws," he said. "No wonder he can catch turkeys and pigs, they're like daggers."

"That's how he hooks those trout and flips them up on the bank," Aidan said.

Mike finished up his work and they filled a pan with water and left it near the cat. Then they backed down the hill and sat down against some trees to watch it wake up. After a while it began to move and tried to raise its head. It lay a few minutes longer and then rolled up to its haunches. It looked around confused, saw the water and leaned forward and took a drink.

"He looks fine," Mike said.

The cat looked down at them and licked its face. Then it got up and walked back farther into the cave.

"He probably is still groggy, and feels like another nap,"

Dylan said.

"Well, I guess we should let him be for a while."

They got up and hiked back to Mike's house. When they got there Mike made them some food and they all ate and rested.

"You know," Aidan said. "We need to keep other people out of this valley so no one finds out about him. You know for sure, if people find out a cougar lives here, some dumb head will come out and try to catch him or shoot at him."

"You're right," Dylan said. "Some dope like Clifford."

"Well, it would take a lot of signs but we can post the whole thing. Aidan your family owns the whole valley except this part where my land joins it. We can start at the other end and put up posters every fifty feet or so keeping people out."

'Man that would take a lot of signs," Dylan said.

"Probably a couple hundred," Mike agreed. "But I'm willing to pay for signs if we can find someone to put them up."

He looked at the boys and grinned.

"What ya got planned for the rest of the week?" Dylan asked.

"How about we start on the weekend? This is the last week of school so we can start Saturday and work on it until we finish. With checking on Spirit and watching his healing, we're gonna be busy for a while anyway," Aidan said.

"Sounds like a plan," Dylan said.

"I'll call the Ace Hardware and order the signs. I'm sure they have some but I doubt they have that many. I'll tell them you guys are going to pick them up. Get a few pounds of roofing nails and you can work on it as you have time. I doubt many people would be in the valley this time of year so as long as we get it done by hunting season we'll be ok."

"Unless a turkey hunter sneaks in there," Dylan said.

"Oh crap, I forgot all about turkey hunting," Aidan said. "I've got to get out there in the morning and try to find that big multiple bearded tom again. After what happened today I doubt he'll roost up on the hill where he was the past few days. I'm going to have to start all over."

"Let's come out and I'll stay with you in the tent tonight. We can sit out in the valley in a couple of places and listen to hear if we can find out where they're going to roost," Dylan said.

"Yeah that sounds like a good idea."

Mike smiled at them. "You guys have been friends a long time?"

"We've been friends since we were babies I guess. I don't ever remember not being friends," Aidan said.

"We've never had a fight either," Dylan said. "Oh I'm not saying we've not disagreed but it's never come to anything serious.

"You guys are pretty close, I can tell that."

"Sometimes… it's almost scary," Dylan said grinning.

 **Chapter 34**

The boys went back home and let their parents know what they had in mind for the evening, letting out the part about Spirit. Mike sent a couple of rings of bologna with them and after getting some food together for themselves they went back to the valley late in the afternoon.

"Let's fill a jug with water and hike up and check on Spirit," Aidan suggested.

Dylan filled a jug from the stream and Aidan chopped up a ring of bologna and they hiked up to the cliffs. They didn't try to be too quiet and wanted the cat to know they were coming so he wouldn't get surprised. When they were quite a way down the hill yet they saw him looking over the ledge.

They hiked up the hill and smiled as they saw his tail whipping back and forth like he was glad to see them. They moved out onto the ledge and sat down a little way from the cat.

"Take a piece and give it to him," Aidan said.

Dylan reached into the bag and took a piece of bologna out. When the cat saw it his tail really began to whip back and forth. Dylan held it out and he took it and gulped it down.

"I guess his appetite is ok," Dylan said grinning.

Aidan handed him the sack of meat and reached for the water pan while Dylan fed the cat. Aidan dumped the old water and rinsed out the pan and then filled it with the fresh water.

The cat got up and took a long drink and then looked up at them, his muzzle dripping.

"How you feeling boy?" Aidan asked.

The cat licked its face and stood there as if he was waiting for something else. Aidan raised his hand and touched him on the side of the face. Spirit leaned into his hand and pushed against it, asking for more. Aidan turned to Dylan, "It just keeps getting better and better."

Aidan petted Spirit for a while and then looked at his side. It seemed to be scabbed over well and looked pretty good.

"Well Spirit, we're going down now. We'll see you again tomorrow boy."

They got up and moved back down the ledge and down the hill. The cat watched them go all the way down to the bottom.

"I keep wondering if we're doing the right thing making friends with him," Dylan said.

"I've thought that too," Aidan replied. "He might think all humans are like that and then walk right up to someone with a deer rifle someday and get himself killed."

"Yeah, well, we have to hope that isn't going to happen I guess."

They went back to the camp and ate their supper. Then just before dusk they split up and one went north and the other south to listen for turkeys going to their roost.

"You'll know if they're around you," Aidan said. "When they fly up into the trees they crash through the branches and make a heck of a racket."

The sky was still fairly bright when Dylan heard a crashing sound from up the hill and to the left of him. He looked and soon saw one of the toms fly up onto a branch in a big oak tree. Then the bird flew up a little farther and landed on another branch. When the first one was well up in the tree the second tom flew up. Soon the third tom did the same.

"Well, I know where they are," Dylan said to himself.

When he got back to the camp Aidan had the fire stoked up and was sitting poking it with a stick.

"Well? Did you hear anything?"

"I know right where they are," Dylan said.

"Did you hear them or see them too?"

"I heard them first but then saw them and it was the toms. I put a stick right on the stream bank to mark the spot where we should go up the hill. I think we can get up a little draw and get pretty close."

Aidan grinned. "Good work Dyl. You'd make somebody a good guide someday."

They sat and talked and poked the fire for an hour or so until it started getting cold. They did their business and crawled into the tent, undressed and slipped into their sleeping bags. Aidan set his alarm.

"Aidan, do you really think we can keep Spirit a secret?"

"I don't know Dylan. If he is happy here in the valley he'd have no reason to go elsewhere where somebody might see him, but he's a wild cat, he might just decide to go on a journey someday and we can't do much about it."

"Yeah that's what I was thinking too. Well for the time being, we're two lucky guys. You talk about a strange pet jeez we got the prize for that one."

They hunkered down in their sleeping bags and soon Dylan was snoring. Aidan lay there awake for a while thinking about the cat and how strange it was to have it as a friend. "Most kids have a dog or a cat and we've got a cougar. That's bizarre."

Soon he drifted off to sleep with the vision of Spirit leaning into his hand as he petted him.

Chapter 35

While the boys slept, the cat was on the prowl. He was hungry and found a ready meal that he could take with little effort.

A mile south of the valley the cat made its way through a hole in a chicken wire fence and into the chicken yard of the small house at the edge of town. The smell of live birds was heavy on the air. He crept across the chicken yard to the small door in front of the chicken coop. There was a little ramp leading up into the coop where the chickens came in and out during the day.

He looked toward the house and could hear the noises of the humans talking. The yard was dark and quiet. His hunger emboldened him and smelling the live birds caused him to climb up the little ramp.

He stuck his head in the door and the chickens began to cluck and shuffle around. They were sitting on roosts and had been sleeping quietly until they sensed the cat in their house. In a quick step he moved inside and one of the hens began to cluck loudly and flap her wings. The wings triggered the cat and he jumped up and took the squalling hen off her perch. Now all the hens were squawking and squalling. There were feathers flying as the birds began flying around the coop. Some of the chickens began running all over the place.

The cat had the hen by the neck and she was dead, hanging from his jaws. Suddenly a light came on from the house. A human began to shout. The cat scampered out of the little door and headed across the chicken pen. A woman came running toward the chicken pen with a broom, yelling and screaming.

"Drop her, drop her! Help he's got Blanch!"

The cat found the hole in the wire and scrambled through it and into the woods.

The woman was joined by a man and a boy. "It was a big cat," the woman said.

"What do you mean? Like a big tomcat?" the man asked.

"No not a tomcat, a huge cat, like a lion."

"Like a lion, are you sure?" the man asked.

"Yes, I saw it with my own eyes, it had one of the chickens in its mouth. It was Blanch," the woman wailed.

"Holy smokes," the boy said.

"What do you mean?"

"I've heard rumors at school."

 **Chapter 36**

It was dark and cold when Aidan's alarm woke the boys. They weren't real happy about getting out of their warm sleeping bags but after laying and yawning for a while Dylan let a huge fart and that got them moving. Aidan grabbed his clothes and climbed out the door gasping for air.

"Holy smokes, you need to go to a doctor and see what's dead inside you," he said as Dylan came from the tent laughing.

"That's my patented wake up call," he said.

They dressed and picked up the gun and one turkey decoy. Since they didn't know for sure where the hens were, they'd use a decoy to try to lure the toms to their hiding spot.

They walked up the valley by starlight and Dylan found his marker stick. Then he led the way up the hill to where he thought they should sit. When they got about half way up Dylan stepped close and said, "The toms are right over there," he said pointing to the big oak. "I think if we sit here someplace they'll hear us if we call and if we set out that decoy they'll see it and come over."

"Sounds like a plan, let me find a good place to sit and then you can place the decoy."

Aidan looked for a couple of wide trees that were fairly close together and walked over and cleaned the leaves and sticks from beneath them carefully so not to make a lot of noise. Then he sat by one and motioned for Dylan to put the decoy a little farther up the hill. When Dylan looked back again Aidan motioned ok and Dylan stuck the decoy into the dirt and came over and sat by the second tree.

"So, now we wait," he said.

They were both wearing full camouflage including head nets that just let their eyes show. Even though a blind was an added comfort it wasn't necessary as long as they remained perfectly still once a turkey was in sight.

The woods slowly came alive and the light grew until the sky became a medium blue, when the first hen yelped from a tree just up the hill behind them.

"Perfect," Aidan whispered.

Soon the hens began to yelp and the toms began gobbling. A bit later they heard them fly down to the ground. Aidan had his diaphragm turkey call in his mouth and made a yelp on it. One of the toms answered immediately.

"Ooh, a hot one," Dylan whispered.

Aidan waited a minute and then yelped again a little more aggressively. The tom answered again. A minute later the tom gobbled again and he was much closer.

"He's coming!" Dylan said.

Suddenly Aidan could see something bluish white moving on the hillside. The tom's head was all bright and glowing in the dim light as he waddled forward in full strut toward the first hen of the day. Aidan had the gun resting on his knee. He moved it up just a few inches and clicked off the safety. The tom came over a small rise and there he was, looking huge, moving right at them.

"Let him come," Dylan whispered.

Aidan didn't have to be told. They'd always been of the opinion that as long as a turkey was moving toward you, let him keep on coming. That way it was farther for him to run away if you missed the first shot.

The huge tom came within fifteen yards and stopped. He turned all the way around displaying his wares to the hen decoy he thought would come running to him. One of the subordinate toms walked up next to the big guy and stood there looking around.

"That smaller one is in the way," Aidan whispered.

The big tom gobbled again. When the hen didn't respond he slowly waddled toward her. The subordinate tom stayed where he was. The big tom walked around behind the hen and dropped his feathers to mount her and breed her.

Boom! Aidan's gun roared and the tom dropped like it had been run over. Its wings flapped and its feet ran through the air but it wasn't going anywhere. Aidan and Dylan jumped to their feet and ran to the bird.

"Holy Maloney, look at that thing," Dylan said looking down at the huge tom.

"Jeez, I've never seen a turkey like that. He's huge."

They knelt beside the bird and turned him so they could see his beards.

"One, look at that long one, it's close to a foot long, two, three, four, five, six, and one little one, seven, jeez Dyl he's got seven beards!"

"Amazing, look at the spurs, they're well over an inch long," Dylan said lifting up one leg.

"The other one is missing," Aidan said. They looked closer and sure enough the second spur was broken off right at the leg.

Aidan lifted the bird. "Holy smokes he's got to be well over twenty pounds."

Dylan clapped his pal on the back. "You did good man... of course you had a heck of a guide."

Aidan put his arm around Dylan's shoulder. "That I did, the best guide," he said smiling.

"Let's get a picture," Dylan said.

They posed the tom with his wings spread and his beards separated. Then Aidan knelt behind him and spread his tail feathers. Dylan took his pocket camera and sat it on a log and framed the picture and then set the timer. He ran back and knelt to the left of Aidan and put his arm around his buddy's shoulder. They both broke out in cheesy grins just as the camera snapped.

"That's one we'll look at when we're old men," Aidan said.

"No doubt. Now we better get this big boy back. One of us has to run up and feed and water Spirit and the other can pull the insides out of this guy and get the camp ready. We've got to go to school today, it's the last day of the year," Dylan said.

"Would you rather get the camp ready or go up and see Spirit?"

Dylan grinned. "I'll take care of camp. You and Spirit have a kind of a special bond, go for it."

Aidan hoisted the big turkey up over his shoulder and the two friends walked down the hill... two happy hunters.

Chapter 37

"We've got plenty of time," Aidan said when they got back to camp. Our turkey hunt only took a little over half an hour."

Dylan nodded. "Yeah you're right, I didn't realize it was still so early. Maybe I'll fix up some breakfast while you're up feeding Spirit and after I get the turkey gutted."

Aidan grabbed the bag of bologna chunks and went to the stream and filled the canteen. Then he jogged up the valley to the cliffs and started up the hill.

Whew," he thought to himself. "That pig is beginning to stink. We should bring a shovel up here and bury the darn thing later."

When he got three quarters of the way up the hill he was surprised to see Spirit coming down toward him. He stopped and waited for the cat.

"Hey boy, you must be feeling better," he said as he squatted down and the cat came up and rubbed against him like a housecat would do. "I bet you're hungry too," he said.

He opened the bag of bologna and started feeding the cat. He was obviously hungry, gobbling up each chunk as it was offered. It didn't take long for the bologna to disappear.

"Sorry Spirit, that's all I have. I guess we're going to have to start bringing more food to you."

"Try this," a voice said.

Aidan looked down the hill and there was Dylan. "I pulled the insides out of that big bird and this gizzard is the size of a small roast. I figured he's used to eating raw meat anyway, why throw it away?"

The cat saw Dylan and loped down the hill to him. Dylan looked up at Aidan and grinned from ear to ear. "Maybe he likes me like he likes you after all," he said.

"He likes gizzard too," Aidan laughed.

Dylan held out the big chunk of meat and the cat grabbed it and began chewing chunks of it down until it was all gone. Then he and Dylan walked side by side up to Aidan.

"His side looks real good. His wound is all dried up and looks like its healing. Doesn't seem like he's limping much now either," Dylan said.

"I think he's recovering pretty well. I'm going up and re-fill his water pan but I'd bet he'll be out on his own soon."

The boys petted Spirit for a while and then started back to the camp. The cat stood and watched them go down the hill and then he climbed back up to his ledge and lay down for a nap, his stomach full.

The boys closed up the camp and headed back home. They stopped at Dylan's so he could shower and change for school. While he was cleaning up his mom and dad were quite impressed with the huge turkey. Then Dylan borrowed his dad's pickup and they went to Aidan's so he could get ready. Aidan's mom said she'd pick the bird and finish cleaning it. Aidan made sure she saved the wings and tail and beards so he could have them made into a trophy mount by a taxidermist.

They headed to school, and made it just as the bell rang. There wasn't much to do in school except get checked out from each class. The morning passed quickly and they were in the cafeteria eating their last school lunch of the year when Sonny Summers came up and sat across from them at the table.

"How's your arm?" he said to Dylan.

"Healed," Dylan answered gruffly.

"Hey, I'm really sorry about that. Clifford decided to play a joke on you and it got way out of hand. I should have warned you and I'm real sorry about it."

"Don't worry, it's over," Dylan said.

"Good. Hey I wanted to talk to you about something else though."

"What's that Sonny?"

"I know Clifford was talking about you guys and some cat that you were looking for. I think it might have visited our chicken house last night."

Aidan looked at Sonny with alarm. "What are you talking about?"

"Well last night late we heard a racket coming from my mom's chicken house. Those chickens are like her kids. She frets and stews over them and treats them like pets. Actually it's kind of embarrassing."

"What about a cat?"

"Well, like I said, we heard this racket and mom went running for the chicken house and started screaming about a huge cat that was killing one of her favorite hens. She was yelling, 'It's got Blanch, help, help'"

"Blanch?"

"Yeah the chicken... Mom's a little goofy like I said."

"So did you see the cat?"

"No dad and I were just coming out of the house. Mom said it was a huge tan colored cat and it took Blanch with it through a hole in the fence."

Aidan looked at Dylan with a worried look. "This was last night?"

Sonny nodded. "Clifford thinks you guys have some big cat someplace and I thought this might have been your cat out hunting."

"You live almost right in town. You must live a good mile from our place," Dylan said.

"Yeah, I know. I'm not saying anything about you and some

cat, I just thought if you're looking for a cat this might be it."

"Well we're not really looking for a cat," Aidan said. "We heard rumors and were just interested in it."

"That stupid Clifford…..he heard you talking about a cat and of course he'd think something silly like that," Sonny said grinning. Well anyway, the memorial service for Blanch will be tomorrow," he laughed. "Just kidding."

He got up and walked away.

Dylan looked at Aidan. "That couldn't have been Spirit. He wouldn't travel a mile for a chicken when he had bologna delivered to him would he?"

"I hardly think so," Aidan replied. "But this is the second "big cat" that's attacked something in the area in the past week or so. It makes me wonder if Spirit is the only big cat around here."

"We better talk to Mike."

 Chapter 38

The boys stopped at the Ace Hardware to pick up the NO TRESSPASSING signs. The owner had them all ready for them.

"Mike had me put in two slap staplers too," the man said. "These are staplers like many roofers use to put down tar paper on the roof. You fill them with staples and then just slap them onto the sign and it staples it to the tree or post. It'll save you a lot of time. They're like a hammer with a staple in the end."

The boys were impressed with the idea and took the box of signs, the two slap staplers and several boxes of staples with them. When they got home they called Mike.

"We've got the signs and stuff," Aidan said. "We're going to start tomorrow. I got that big tom this morning so we're done turkey hunting for now. Dylan's season isn't until a week from Wednesday, so we can spend plenty of our time on the signs."

"I heard you shoot this morning pretty early," Mike said. "You must have gotten him right off the roost."

Aidan told Mike the story and then told him about how Spirit was up and moving around.

"That's good. I'm sure he'll be ok now. You guys can probably stop worrying about feeding him. He probably can manage on his own."

"Well, we stopped and got a couple of packages of wieners, so we might as well use them up," Aidan said.

Mike laughed. "And it's fun feeding him and messing around with him too isn't it?"

Aidan had to admit that was a big part of it. "Hey Mike a kid at school talked to us today about a big cat that raided their chicken coop and stole a hen last night. He said his mom saw a huge cat. Do you think it's possible Spirit was a mile from here?"

"I doubt it very much. Why would he go steal a chicken when he's been getting wieners and bologna?

"That's the second time somebody's asked us about a big cat in that area. There wouldn't be another cougar would there be?"

"Boy... that would really be a surprise to me if there were. Spirit is one of a kind. I really doubt another cougar found his way here. I've been watching his transmitter and he hasn't moved more than a hundred yards from his cave. It's not him."

"Well that's good to know."

They hung up with plans to stop at Mike's place the next day and took a package of wieners and rode back to the valley. Instead of stopping at the camp they drove up the valley and stopped below the cliffs. Before they got off the 4 wheeler Spirit was loping down the hillside to them.

They got off the vehicle and he began rubbing up against them and purring like some old house cat. Aidan opened the package of wieners and they took turns feeding them to him.

"He's like a dang house cat," Dylan said as Spirit prodded his hand for a wiener he was hiding.

Aidan couldn't keep the smile off his face. "I hope we're doing the right thing though Dyl. This is something we'll never forget but I hope it doesn't take his fear of humans away and make him vulnerable in the future."

They spent an hour with the cat just fooling around with him in the grass. He was obviously very glad to see them and enjoyed their company. Finally they decided it was time to go home, so they got on the vehicle and said goodbye. The cat sat and watched them as they drove down the valley.

"I think he's pretty well recovered," Dylan said over his shoulder.

"Yeah, but it's worth a few wieners to be able to play with him isn't it?

Saturday morning they loaded up the signs and staplers and headed down the highway to where the road met their property.

They pulled off the road and stopped.

"I'll let you out here and I'll drive down the ridge a quarter of a mile or so and leave the vehicle. I'll start there and work north. When you get to the vehicle, take it about a quarter of a mile past where you find it and do the same. We can leap frog all the way down this side of the valley. When we get to Mike's land we can go as far as his driveway and then stop and see him. It'll be about lunch time then and with any luck we can get a free lunch," Aidan said.

"I'm hungry already," Dylan said grabbing a stack of signs. "See ya later."

Aidan drove along the line fence and found a good place to park. He took a pack of signs and his stapler and started stapling a sign to a tree about every fifty feet. A while later he heard Dylan going past on the 4 wheeler. When he got to the machine he started it and drove to Mike's driveway. He put up several signs and then saw Dylan coming up through the woods.

"How'd it go?" he asked.

"Not bad. The mosquitoes were kind of bad down in the woods but it's pretty easy with these slap things. That was a good idea."

"Well, it's almost noon, let's go see Mike," Aidan said.

As they drove up over the top of the hill and saw Mike's house. They also saw smoke coming from his grill and smelled a very good aroma.

"Mike must have read our minds," Dylan grinned.

Chapter 39

"I figured you might show up when you needed feeding," Mike said as the boys got off the 4 wheeler."

"You know us pretty well," Dylan said, "What's cooking?"

"Oh I thought BBQ ribs and potato salad and baked beans might be ok?"

"Oh man, lead me to it!" Dylan said.

They sat at a picnic table in Mike's yard and ate. The boys went through the ribs like they hadn't eaten in a week.

"Jeez, these are the best ribs I've ever had," Dylan said gnawing the last of the meat from a bone. "And these beans, whooie, you don't want to be around me in about a half an hour."

"I plan to be far away," Aidan said. "I've been around you after beans too many times."

"So Mike, is Spirit moving around today?"

Mike nodded. "He's been up since dawn. He went down and got a drink and then I watched him stalk a sow with some little pigs. He missed them though. The sow saw him too soon and he's still a little stiff acting. He stopped and fished and caught a nice trout so he's not starving."

"He's quite an amazing thing," Aidan said.

"You guys are getting pretty friendly."

"You saw?"

Mike nodded. "I was watching when you fed him yesterday. He's completely at ease with you two. I've never seen anything like it. I have a friend who lives in Wyoming who has a cat that will come around and sit and watch him when he's out on his ranch. He's told me many times when he's out repairing a fence or rounding up his cattle that he'll look up and there the cat will be, lying on a knoll watching him. But that one has never gotten close enough to be touched. That cat has been there for ten years or more. This guy's ranch is something like 20,000 acres so other than people who are invited on it, no one ever gets close to this cat. He's safe as can be and doesn't do any harm, so they've become kind of friends. A cat that actually is friendly to the point of being petted is very uncharacteristic for this type of animal. To my knowledge it's never happened before. This one is kind of one-of-a-kind cat."

"Do you think he'll be content to stay here from now on?" Aidan asked.

"He has no reason to leave. He's got plenty of food and free delivery service of wieners, and a nice place to live. I'm sure he's as happy as any cougar in the country. Plus he has human friends. He's a very unusual cat," Mike said.

They chatted for a while and Dylan began to pass gas so they thought it'd be a good idea to break up the party. They bid Mike goodbye and thanked him for a great meal and got on the 4 wheeler and took off.

When they got to the property line again they began leapfrogging on around the valley. They planned on going across Mike's property at the head end of the valley and over to the cliff's area. By then they'd be ready for a rest. They could finish the signs the next day.

Aidan let Dylan off, went a ways, left the machine and walked to the fence line and began putting up signs. A while later he heard the vehicle go past. They were getting to the rocky cliff area; the terrain was getting rougher. Aidan back tracked several times when he came to a ditch that ran down over the ridge too deep to cross. It was much slower going here.

When he got to the vehicle he could see signs along the woods for a hundred yards but then they stopped. He drove up that far and stopped to see how Dylan was holding up. He knew he was getting tired and thought maybe they'd quit for the day.

He walked to the last sign on the edge of a deep ditch.

"He must have backtracked rather than go down that ditch," he thought to himself.

Aidan began walking up along the side of the ditch and couldn't see Dylan anywhere.

"Hey Dyl, what're you doing having a nap?"

"Aidan!"

He could hear Dylan's voice coming from up ahead and it sounded like it was at the bottom of the ditch. He walked up and looked over the side.

"What are you doing hiding?"

Dylan was leaning back against a flat slab of rock at the bottom of the ditch. His feet were tucked under him in an uncomfortable looking position. He looked up slowly and by the look in his face Aidan could tell something was very wrong.

"What?"

Dylan eyes moved down and to the left. "Snake!" he said quietly.

Chapter 40

Aidan could see that Dylan was shaking slightly. From the time when they were kids Dylan had always been terrified of snakes. Their first encounter had been when they were around five years old and they had lifted up an old sandbox in the back yard and found a nest of baby garter snakes. The little snakes had scattered in all directions and several of them had crawled across Dylan's bare feet. He had been frightened so badly that he wouldn't go into Aidan's back yard for several years.

Aidan eased up to the edge of the ditch and peered over the side. Dylan motioned with his eyes to the right and Aidan saw the snake. It was thick like a baseball bat and coiled up, its tail sticking up and its head held above the coils, looking directly at Dylan. "Holy smokes, it's a rattle snake Dyl," he whispered.

"I know," Dylan said very quietly. "What am I going to do?"

Aidan could see tears in Dylan's eyes and he was shaking from fear.

"Just stay calm. Let me look this over. Don't worry I'll get you out of there."

Dylan nodded slightly.

The snake was lying at the edge of a flat slab of shale. It looked like it had been under the slab when Dylan got too close and disturbed it. It was only about three feet from his legs.

"Dylan, if I can distract the snake can you get up on that rock above you? Aidan asked.

Dylan looked up at the big rock he was leaning back against, keeping him as far from the snake as possible. He swallowed hard. "I think I can make it up there," he said. "Dang Aidan my legs feel like jello. I've been standing here for almost an hour. I thought you were never coming."

"Flex your knees and toes and try to get some blood flowing into your legs while I move down the ditch a little way and work my way up to you. I'll try to get the snake to turn and look at me and when it does, jump up on that rock. He won't be able to strike you up there."

Dylan nodded.

Aidan carefully backed away from the edge of the ditch. He walked toward the woods and looked for a long stick that would work for his plan. He finally found one with a sharp angled branch on the lower end and picked it up and broke it off about six feed from the end. Then he broke the branch off and he ended up with a stick with a hook on the end. Then he moved downhill about ten yards and looked for a way down into the ditch. He found a place that wasn't too steep and carefully climbed down. He looked around to be sure there weren't any more snakes in the area. Once in the bottom of the ditch he began working his way quietly and carefully up toward Dylan.

He got closer and closer and could hear the snake buzzing. It was getting agitated probably because it heard or felt him walking toward it. It was coiled and had its head up ready to strike.

"Get ready," Aidan whispered.

"Wait, wait" Dylan said.

"What's wrong?

"I gotta........." Dylan let a huge fart.

Aidan began laughing. "Jeez, that'll probably kill the snake."

"Dang I couldn't hold it any longer. I've been holding that for an hour.

"Ok are you ready now?"

Dylan nodded and swallowed.

Aidan inched forward and could see the snake staring at Dylan. He moved the hooked stick closer and closer to the raised head of the snake. When he felt he could hook it he whispered, "Oh Dyl, get ready, in three, two, one."

Aidan hooked the snake with his stick and jerked it back toward him. Dylan sprang up onto the rock like a gazelle and hung on for dear life. The snake was now rattling like crazy and was very angry after being jerked over onto its back. It rolled over on its stomach and came toward Aidan.

He began to back up to get away. The snake was coming much faster than he'd expected it would and he hurried a little too fast and fell backward over a piece of a branch that had fallen into the ditch. The snake was only five feet away and coming fast. Aidan hit the ground on his back and rolled right over in a backward summersault and came right back up onto his feet. He took a couple of strides more and then jumped up onto a slab of rock and climbed up out of the ditch.

Meanwhile Dylan had climbed out onto the other side of the ditch from the rock he had move up onto. They were both safe and the snake was alive and well, even though it was pretty mad.

"Are you ok?" Dylan asked.

Aidan nodded. "I'm quick like a cheetah," he said grinning.

"I'll meet you at the 4 wheeler," Dylan said.

Aidan got to the vehicle first since Dylan had chosen to hike all the way back to the top end of the ditch and then walked down the other side to him. He was grinning when he got to Aidan.

He grabbed his best friend and gave him a huge hug. "Jeez, I owe you one man," he said squeezing his buddy. "I thought I was a goner when that dang snake popped up and started rattling. I couldn't move to get away. I was cornered."

"Sorry I took so long to get here," Aidan said.

"Oh that's ok. I knew you'd get here sooner or later. I was afraid I'd pee my pants or something and make him strike."

They laughed and got a cool drink from the cooler. "Well, I think I've had enough fun for one day," Dylan said.

Aidan nodded. "I guess we learned something today too. I never even thought about there being snakes in these rocks. Now we know and can take a little more care when we're blundering around up here."

"Oh don't worry I'll be watching real close where I step from now on," Dylan said. "Besides, I think I need to go home and change my underwear. That little blast was a tiny bit wet."

Aidan just shook his head.

They loaded up onto the vehicle and started off for home, wiser and more cautious than they'd been on the way to the woods.

Chapter 41

Since it was Sunday the boys made plans to go and try to finish up the signs after church. They figured it was not a good idea to skip out and then have to face the wrath of their mothers. Aidan picked up Dylan after they'd gotten home and changed and they took the 4 wheeler back to where they'd left off.

"If it's ok with you, I'll take the vehicle and go on down the ridge a little way and start. You can start here in the snake area," Dylan said.

Aidan grinned. "Don't want to meet your scaly friend again?"

"Never."

They began working along the fence line and about three hours later they could see the highway. They worked together at the entrance to the valley, putting up signs about every ten feet.

"Now, if anyone says they didn't see a sign, we'll know they're blind," Aidan said.

"Let's finish up and take a run in and see if Spirit's around," Dylan said.

They worked their way back to the highway and put up the last sign about fifty feet from where they'd put the first one the day before.

"Jeez, that was a job," Dylan said.

"Well at least we can hope it keeps people out," Aidan answered.

They got on the vehicle and drove back to the cut and into the valley. As they drove down the middle of the valley to their campsite Dylan tapped Aidan on the shoulder. He nodded to the left.

"Look who's waiting for us."

There lying on the grass a short way from their tent was the cat. His tail began to switch back and forth when he saw them coming. He got to his feet and stood there watching as they drove up and shut off the machine.

"Hey Spirit," Aidan said as he got off the vehicle.

The cat came bounding over to them and began to purr loudly as they petted him.

"Un-freaking-real," Dylan said.

Suddenly the cat turned and ran back to where he'd been lying and picked up a trout from the grass and turned and brought it to the boys. He dropped it on the grass and looked up at them.

"Oh my gosh, he brought us a fish," Aidan said.

"I can't believe that," Dylan said smiling. He reached out and rubbed the side of the cat's face.

"Do we have anything left in the lunch cooler?" Aidan asked.

Dylan took the straps off the little cooler on the back of the 4 wheeler and opened it. "We've got half a sandwich and a brownie," he said.

Aidan shrugged. "Try it."

Dylan took the sandwich out and the cat's ears perked up when he saw it. Dylan held it out and the cat sniffed it and then took it carefully from his fingers. It laid the sandwich on the ground and pulled at the bread until it came off and then ate the ham inside. Dylan held out the brownie but the cat sniffed it and turned away.

"Doesn't like sweets," Dylan said. "He must be watching his figure."

"Pick up the fish and put it in the cooler," Aidan said.

"You want to take it home?"

"Well he brought it for us. We should take it even though we're not going to eat it. It looks kind of dried out. He probably caught it quite a while ago but I want him to think we're going to eat it. After all he brought it to us as a gift."

155

Dylan picked up the fish and said, "Good boy," and dropped it into the cooler and strapped it down.

The cat seemed very pleased with himself.

"Well we should get going. Mom has a big supper planned and if I'm late she'll be unhappy," Dylan said.

"Yeah me too... well boy," he said stroking the cat "we have to go. You be good and stay here in the valley."

They got on the vehicle and drove toward the entrance. Aidan looked over his shoulder and Spirit was sitting by their tent watching them.

"Hey Dyl, I don't think we have to worry about anyone stealing our camping gear from now on."

Dylan laughed. "Wouldn't it be fun to see Clifford sneak in there and begin loading stuff up and turn around and see Spirit standing there watching him?"

"Oh man, I'd pay to see that."

 Chapter 42

The next day Mike called Aidan just after breakfast.

"I was wondering if you and Dylan might be interested in some work now that school is finished for the year," he said.

"Sure, what do you need us to do?"

"Well, I'm finally going to start on the outside of my house. I've ordered new windows and siding and it's going to be delivered today. They've called and will be here about noon and they said I need to have strong backs and weak minds available to help unload... so right away I thought of you and Dylan."

Aidan broke out laughing. "You thought of Dylan you mean. Sure we'll help you, I'll call him and then we'll come up."

"Just wait until we tell Mike about Spirit bringing us a fish," Dylan said as they drove up Mike's rutted driveway. "I'll bet he's never seen anything like that before."

"Everything we do with that cat is something new," Aidan answered.

As they pulled up over the crest of the hill Mike motioned for them to park over by the woods. They parked and walked across the yard.

"The truck will have to have a place to turn around so I wanted you out of the way," he said. "How's our cat?"

They were telling him about the fish when a big flatbed truck groaned up over the hill. The driver was looking a little upset as he pulled to a stop, looked things over and turned around with the back of the truck next to the front yard.

"That's some driveway you've got there," he said as he stepped down from the truck.

"Yeah, it discourages people selling magazine subscriptions," Mike said.

"No doubt, well I've got your materials here, are these guys your helpers?"

"Yep, these are them."

"Well, I'll get up there and start to un-strap the stuff," the man said.

The boys and Mike waited for the windows to be loosened and one by one they carried them and stacked them in the corner of the yard. There was one big double one that took two of them to carry. Then they began taking the half log siding off the truck, one piece at a time. The siding was a pealed log that had been sliced in half making one side flat and the other was left in a natural unfinished state with no bark on it. There were hundreds of pieces of the stuff.

After an hour they took a break. Mike went inside and got sodas for all of them and then after a rest they finished up until the truck was empty. The driver put his straps away, had Mike sign the delivery bill and drove off down the driveway.

"Wow, that's a lot of stuff," Aidan said surveying the stacks of half logs.

"Now the fun starts," Mike said. "All I have to do is remove all the old windows and replace them with new ones and hang all that siding and I'll have my log cabin... inside and out."

"Sounds like a big job for one person," Dylan said.

"That's why I want to hire a couple of helpers," Mike said grinning.

"I see," Aidan said. "Did you have anyone in mind?"

"Well I'm not acquainted with too many people in the area. Do you guys have any suggestions?"

"I know a guy named Clifford," Dylan said laughing.

They all laughed and Mike said, "I'll give you ten bucks an hour, and feed you well."

"You've got two hired hands," Aidan said and Dylan nodded in agreement.

"Great, now before we get all crazy about work, how about we take the rest of the afternoon off and... oh go cat watching."

There were grins all around.

Mike went inside and got a small cooler with cold pop inside and a sack of sandwiches he'd made before the boys arrived and they hiked to the point and sat down to watch the valley.

There were some ducks on the pond and the geese were swimming around with about a dozen little yellow puff balls swimming after them. Somewhere off on the right a hen turkey yelped a few times.

"Pretty place, isn't it?" Mike said.

"It's just like a little piece of heaven," Aidan said. "A lot of people wouldn't think twice about it but Dylan and I have grown up in that valley. I don't know what I'd do if somehow we had to stop going there."

Mike nodded. "That's how I felt when I looked at this property and saw the valley was a part of it. I knew this was where I was supposed to be."

"Mike, do you think we're making a mistake by making friends with Spirit?" Dylan asked. "I mean, if he thinks all humans are like us and he goes out of the valley and walks up to someone, he might get shot."

"That's crossed my mind many times," Mike said, "but I don't know how you could have done anything different. It was the cat who decided to become friends. You guys just were there and for some reason he decided you were ok."

"Yeah, you're right but it bothers us that something bad

might happen to him because of not being afraid of humans," Aidan said.

"We just have to keep an eye on him and if something happens we might have to step in. I guess for now we should just enjoy the way things are going."

They sat until late afternoon but didn't see the cat. Finally they got up and hiked back to the house. Aidan and Dylan made plans to come back about nine in the morning and they'd bring hammers and a few other small tools with them.

In the valley the geese retired to the bulrushes with their brood, the ducks settled in the middle of the pond to sleep and the turkeys flew up to their roosts.

Spirit appeared from the cliffs and stood on a rock surveying his domain. Then he started down the ridge to the north... out of the valley.

 Chapter 43

That night the cat struck the chicken house again. He crawled through the same hole in the fence that had given him access to the easy meal the first time he'd been there. He crept quietly to the chicken house and looked at the chicken door which was open as it had been the first time.

Inside the chickens began to cluck and move around, alerted to the presence of the cat. One hen began to cluck loudly and began flapping her wings. That action set off the cat and he slipped through the little door and grabbed the hen off the roost. She screamed loudly and the rest of the flock began screeching and flapping around inside the coop. The one rooster began to yelp and scream and began crowing.

The yard light came on and the back door of the house opened.

"That cat is back!" a woman's voice screamed.

The cat hurried out the chicken door and headed for the opening in the fence. The woman from the house was at the gate to the chicken yard with a broom, screaming at the top of her lungs.

She made it through the gate and ran toward the cat as he scurried through the hole in the fence and ran for the woods, a chicken in his jaws.

"Shoot, shoot," the woman screamed.

A second person came out the door and raised a shotgun. He swung it toward the cat just as it disappeared into the tall grass at the edge of the woods.

"No! No! He got Milly!"

The woman was crying and screaming at the boy who was carrying the shotgun. "Why didn't you shoot him? What were you waiting for?"

"I couldn't see him well enough. He was almost in the woods when I got here."

"I'm calling the sheriff. This is going to stop one way or the other!" the woman yelled. She stomped into the house while the boy stood there looking towards the woods.

"I gotta talk to Aidan and Dylan," he said to himself.

Meanwhile half a mile away a flock of sheep grazed in a pasture near the edge of the hill. There were twelve sheep and four lambs that had been born in the past three days. The little lambs were hanging together while their mothers and the rest of the adult sheep grazed and some slept.

Suddenly the silent scene erupted with screams and bleats from the sheep and little lambs. A dark shape raced toward the group of lambs and grabbed one by the neck and turned and ran for the woods. The mother sheep called and called but her lamb was gone and there was nothing she could do about it.

The remaining sheep were skittish the rest of the night, huddling together, but their attacker was long gone. It struck and then went home... back to the valley where it lived.

Chapter 44

Aidan was just finishing up breakfast when there was a knock at the door. His mom went to answer it and soon came back with Sonny Summers trailing behind her.

"Sonny?" Aidan said. "Um, what are you doing here?"

"I'm sorry to bother you but I need to talk to you."

"What about?" Aidan said suspiciously.

Sonny looked to see if Aidan's mom was near. "The cat," he said quietly.

"Mom, I'm done, I'm going out to talk to Sonny," Aidan said.

They walked out to the front yard and Aidan said, "Ok let's hear it."

"Well, remember a while back a big cat took Blanch?"

Aidan looked confused.

"Blanch was one of my ma's chickens. Well last night it came back and took another one. She's about fit to be tied. She's going to the sheriff today and she's on the warpath. I know you and Dylan aren't saying anything but Clifford swears you two were talking about a big cat and I'm wondering if you know anything about it."

Aidan felt a chill run down his back. "Sonny, you gotta promise me this is going to stay with us, you can't say a word to Clifford."

"I promise," Sonny said.

"Ok, well Clifford is right. There's a cougar living in our valley. We ran into it earlier in the spring and now it's pretty friendly with us. We're trying to keep people out so no one sees it and tries to hurt it."

"But is it safe for you guys to be near it?"

"That's the strange part. The thing has decided we're his

friends. He comes to our campground and well, you're not going to believe this, but he eats hot dogs from our hands."

"No way!"

Aidan nodded. "He has plenty of food so I really don't think he'd travel a mile and a half to your place for a chicken. And besides that, the last time you lost a chicken he was hurt. He got into a fight with a big wild boar and had a shoulder injury. It kept him pretty quiet for a week and that was when you lost that first chicken, whatever its name was."

"Blanche."

"Ok, Blanche. I don't think your cat and our cat are the same cat."

"I just got a glimpse of it and it wasn't as big as a cougar," Sonny said. "I'd say it was about the size of a beagle."

"Well Spirit is five feet long with a three foot tail. He probably weighs a hundred and fifty pounds."

"This cat is lots smaller than that."

"Well that's good to know. So maybe we're ok."

"I don't know. My ma is really worked up about it. She likes those stupid chickens better than she likes me and my dad. If Clifford hears about this second chicken he'll put her on the trail of your cat... for sure."

"Oh man, he can be a real pain in the butt," Aidan said.

"I'll see if I can cool things down. I won't say a word about your cougar."

"Thanks Sonny, I appreciate it."

Sonny got in his beat up old pickup and drove away.

Aidan took the 4 wheeler over to Dylan's and told him what had happened. "Oh boy, that's not good," Dylan said.

"We better tell Mike."

"I can't get the pickup today. We'll have to take the 4 wheeler up through the valley and then walk up to Mike's," Dylan said.

They got onto Aidan's 4wheeler and started for the valley. As they got to the entrance they slowed down, passed through and headed up the valley toward their camp.

"What's that by the tent?" Dylan said pointing to their campsite.

"Looks like a tee shirt or something. It's something white."

They got closer and suddenly they both realized what the white object was. "Oh no," Aidan said.

A dead lamb lay next to the tent. Its throat was all bloody but otherwise it was untouched.

"Another present," Dylan said looking down at the little lamb.

"Oh Dyl, this is bad. This is real bad."

"We've got to hide this so no one sees it if they come into the valley," Aidan said.

They looked around and decided on putting the lamb behind a pile of brush and camouflaging it with sticks and leaves. They looked up and down the valley but Spirit was nowhere to be seen.

"He's probably sleeping in late," Aidan said. "After his hunting trip last night he's probably tired. Oh man we better get up to Mike's fast."

They rode up the valley and parked below the ridge at Mike's place. They hiked up the trail as fast as they could go. They were both huffing pretty hard when they came out of the woods into Mike's yard. Mike was just about ready to remove an old window that he'd loosened from the frame.

"Ah you got here at just the right time," he said smiling.

"Mike we've got a problem," Aidan said.

Mike left the window sitting in the frame.

"What's wrong?"

Aidan told him the story he'd heard from Sonny and what they'd found at the campsite.

Mike thought for a bit and then said. "Well, if what Sonny says is accurate, I'd say there's a bobcat around his place raiding the chicken coop. That's probably what took that little dog a while back too. They're not real common in this part of the state

165

but they're fairly common in the north. Most likely one has moved into this area."

"But if his mom gets everyone riled up, our cat is going to be in danger too," Dylan said.

"I agree. And the sheep is a bad deal. I think I know where it came from. I know a guy a ways from here that has a little flock. Obviously Spirit thought he was doing a good thing bringing you a present. I think I can smooth it over with the farmer and pay for the lamb but that's not going to do anything to keep Spirit from going out and getting into more trouble in the future."

"The problem is Sonny's mom and Clifford. They'll get everything stirred up and we're not going to be able to keep them out of the valley," Dylan said.

"What are we going to do?" Aidan asked.

Just then they heard the sound of a car coming up the driveway. They turned and looked as a sheriff's deputy pulled into the yard.

 Chapter 45

Dylan looked at Aidan. "Uh oh."

The deputy got out of the car and walked over to the three of them.

"I'm Deputy Biba, are you Mr. Florian?"

Mike stepped forward and held out his hand. "Yes I'm Mike Florian, pleased to meet you. What can we do for you?"

The deputy turned to the boys. "I think we have a special friend in common."

The boys looked at each other. "I'm not sure I follow you," Aidan said.

"I ran into Tom the UPS man the other day," Biba said, "and he was telling me about his conversation a while back with you boys about an unusual animal you seem to know the whereabouts of."

Suddenly Aidan realized who the deputy was. "You're the officer Tom told us about that saw the… the cougar?"

Biba smiled. "I'm the guy. It was seven or eight months ago. I farm as well as work for the sheriff and I was at home and in the barn one morning and my wife called me on the barn phone from the house. I was standing there talking to her and I looked out the milk house window and there was a cougar walking through my barnyard. I told her to look but by the time she believed me and actually went to the window the cat jumped over the barnyard fence and sprinted off into the woods. She never did believe me but I'm as sure of what I saw as I am of you guys."

"It's kind of an eye opener the first time isn't it?" Mike said.

Biba turned to him. "You've seen him too I take it?"

"He lives in the valley down there," Mike said pointing to the ridge. "The boys and I have been watching him all spring. Actually he's become pretty good friends with these boys too."

"As in how?" Biba asked.

"As in he'll eat hot dogs out of our hand," Aidan said.

Biba shook his head. "Amazing. Well I knew he was around here someplace and this is a good place for him. But we've had some incidents that seem to point that he's been out attacking some of the local folk's animals."

"Someone complained?" Dylan asked.

"Do you know Mrs. Summers?" Biba asked.

Dylan shook his head. "No, I've not had the pleasure but I know her son. He told us it was a cat but not a cougar."

"She calls it a giant killer cat," the deputy said with a half grin.

"Have you been there at the scene of the crime?" Mike asked.

"Yes and I've seen the hole in the fence that the killer cat came through," the deputy said.

"How big was that hole?"

He held up his hands making a hole about a foot square. "Not big enough for a cougar," he said.

"I think there's a bobcat in the area," Mike said. "I'm a trained biologist and this attack sounds exactly like the predation a bobcat would be involved in. They go for small things, chickens, little dogs, rabbits. A cougar would take a chicken but he wouldn't travel a mile and a half for one."

"That's what I thought too," the deputy said, "but Mrs. Summers is a determined lady. She's called each and every county board member and is demanding a task force be formed to bring this "wanton killer" to justice."

"Oh boy," Aidan said. "So what's going to happen?"

"Right now the sheriff is going to try to placate her with an in-depth investigation and hopefully that will do it. But I doubt it. Anyone who names her chickens is... well a bit on a different page than most of us."

The boys laughed. "If she's anything like her son she's a

dandy," Dylan said.

"There is a problem that I know is going to show up though," Aidan said.

"What's that?" Mike asked.

"Sonny's best buddy Clifford knows about the cat too. At least he has a good idea it's here. As soon as he gets wind of Sonny's mom's crusade he'll spill his guts to her and she'll be here demanding to look in the valley for her chicken killer."

"Well then we have to do something about the cat before she gets that far," Dylan said.

"What can we do?" Aidan asked.

"Deputy Biba, what are your thoughts?" Mike asked.

"Well, I'd like to see the thing left alone. It's a beautiful animal and I see no reason to do it harm. But I'm not the one who's going to decide. I think I can slow things down for a few days but if Mrs. Summers is as adamant as she seems to be, things might get ugly."

"Stall as long as you can," Mike said. "I have to make a couple of phone calls. I think I may have a solution to this."

Deputy Biba nodded. "I'll keep in touch. If I can do anything to help, let me know. I'd like to see this cat live a long happy life."

The deputy drove off and the boys and Mike stood there watching him go. "Well, why don't you two finish taking that window out and I'll make some phone calls. I might have an idea... but I don't think you'll like it."

 **Chapter 46**

The boys finished taking the window out of the house and Mike called the farmer where he thought the lamb came from and made an appointment to see him in a short while. He showed the boys what to do to put the new window in the hole in the house and drove off to fix the dead lamb problem.

The boys followed Mike's instructions and had the new window installed, plumbed and nailed into the hole in a short time. They were pretty proud of themselves since they'd never done anything like that before. When they finished they sat and waited for Mike for a while and then Aidan got a piece of paper and wrote him a note telling him they'd be on the point over the valley.

"We might as well sit and watch to see if Spirit is around," Aidan said as they hiked out the point.

They sat down and looked over the valley. There was no sign of the cat.

"I hope he's not out looking for another present for us," Dylan said.

"Jeez, what are we going to do Dyl? Even if Mike fixes the lamb situation Spirit is going to get in trouble and there's nothing we can do to stop it."

"I don't know Aidan, I wish there was some way to keep him in the valley but you know as well as I do that he can come and go as he pleases. One of these days he's going to walk in front of somebody with a gun and that'll be the end of him."

"Oh I've thought of that so many times, I can't sleep some nights thinking of something bad happening to him."

"Look!" Dylan said pointing to the pond.

There were half a dozen ducks feeding in the shallow end of the pond on some aquatic weeds. In the reeds they could see Spirit sneaking up on the ducks. He was crouched down and just moving in slow motion.

"He's going to try for a duck," Dylan said.

Spirit got within a couple of feet of the edge of the reeds when one of the ducks started quacking and making a fuss. The others came alert and started swimming around quacking.

Suddenly the cat pounced at the closest duck. There was a huge splash and when it disappeared the cat was standing belly deep in the water and all the ducks were ten feet away swimming around. Spirit jumped toward the ducks and they scattered as he landed where they'd just been. Again he pounced and the ducks scurried away.

The boys were laughing as they watched the big cat chasing the ducks around on the pond, making a lot of splashes and riling up the mud but not coming close to a duck.

"Oh he's gonna need some hot dogs after this," Aidan laughed.

Spirit chased the ducks around for ten minutes and finally the little flock swam to the deep end of the pond and the game was over. Spirit stood there dripping and watched the ducks swim away. He waded back to shore and shook like a dog. Then he lay down and began licking his feet and legs, cleaning himself.

"Just like a big barn cat," Aidan said.

They watched the cat clean himself all up and then he got up and sauntered over next to the tent, sniffed it and walked up into the woods.

Dylan looked over at his friend and there were tears in Aidan's eyes. "What's wrong?" he asked.

"We're not going to be able to see him and be friends with him soon Dyl. You know as well as I do that this is done."

Dylan nodded. "Yeah, I've felt like that since we found the lamb."

Just then they heard Mike's horn sound on his vehicle so they got up and walked back to the house.

Mike was looking at the window. "Nice job, nice and straight and plumb. You guys might make carpenters yet."

"So how'd it go with the lamb guy?"

"He hadn't even missed it. I told him what had happened and he was very interested in Spirit. He said he'd keep his mouth shut and I told him we'd do everything we could to keep him from killing any more lambs."

"But Mike, what can we do short of caging him up?"

"I have a solution, but I don't think you'll like it much," Mike said.

"What is it?"

"Remember I told you about my friend in Wyoming that had the cougar that hung around? The last I talked to him was last fall and he told me he was afraid this past winter was going to be the last for his cougar. The cat was getting old and was lame. It's been around his ranch for years. Well I called him and his cougar disappeared in January. He found him when the snow melted. He didn't make it through the cold weather."

"So how does that help us?" Dylan asked.

"I told him about Spirit and his troubles with the local folks and my friend said to bring him to Wyoming and he'd give him a home for as long as he lived. There are no other male cougars with a territory there yet. So Spirit could take over the old cat's territory without a lot of fighting with other local cats. He said there are a couple of females in the area that have their territories overlapping the old cat's too."

"You mean we'd take him to Wyoming?"

Mike nodded. "He'd be safe. He'd have his own territory, and a possible female. He could live a long quiet life like a cougar is meant to live. There are only about half a million people in all of Wyoming, so it's not like he'd be a target."

The boys stood there stunned. "I guess you're right, but..." Aidan said.

"I've got to take a walk."

Aidan walked off toward the point and Dylan looked at Mike.

"Just let him go and think about it for a bit," Mike said, "I think he'll see it's the best we can do for the cat."

Chapter 47

"He'll be all right," Dylan said. "He's the one who's spent the most time with Spirit. I know how I feel and its worse with Aidan."

"I'm going to make some calls," Mike said.

Dylan sat in the yard for half an hour and then walked to the point. Aidan was sitting on a stump looking out over the valley. Dylan walked up and Aidan turned toward him, his eyes red.

"It's hard to think about," he said.

Dylan nodded. "I know. But you know as well as I do that he doesn't belong here. He got here by mistake and we were lucky enough to not only get to see him but to actually become friends with him. I'll bet we're the only two teenagers in the world who've been friends with a cougar. At least we're two of very few others."

Aidan nodded. "Yeah, I know how lucky we've been. And I guess deep inside I knew it wouldn't last. It all kind of happened kinda sudden though. I wasn't prepared for it I guess."

"This is a much better solution that him just taking off for who knows where. If some day we just stopped seeing him we'd always wonder what had happened to him. At least we know he'll have his own territory and maybe a girlfriend. He'll be happy there Aidan, that's what counts."

Aidan got up and hugged his friend. "Let's go and see what Mike's cooking up for this little safari."

When they got to the house Mike had a couple of canvass bags packed and ready to go. "I've got what we need for the trip all ready. I called a friend who has a single horse trailer. I'm going to go pick it up and bring it back here. We'll fit it out a little to keep what's inside from being seen by people on the outside. Then all we have to do is get Spirit and convince him to go in and we'll head for Wyoming."

"We need to clear this with our folks," Aidan said.

"Oh I don't plan on leaving today. I figured we can try to leave first thing tomorrow. It's a bit over a thousand miles to Wyoming so we'll be on the road for at least two days getting there. We have to plan for that and for pit stops to let both us and the cat out to move around now and then."

"We better go home and get some things ready. We'll come back in an hour or so and help with the trailer," Aidan said.

He and Dylan hiked down the trail to their vehicle and sped down the valley toward their homes. They explained the trip as an educational opportunity to see a scientist do some studies in Wyoming. They were back at Mike's house waiting when he pulled in with the trailer behind his truck.

They put some plywood over the majority of the spaces in the trailer just letting a few small holes open for fresh air. Then they spread a bail of straw around on the floor and got half a dozen rings of bologna out of Mike's freezer. They stored them in a small cooler and were ready to go.

"I'll come down and pick you guys up around 8am. Then we can go to the valley and park the trailer outside the opening. If you guys can get Spirit to come to you, do you think you can get him inside the trailer?"

"No problem. If we've got bologna he'll do anything we ask," Dylan said.

"Ok, I've called my friend in Wyoming and he's as excited as a kid at Christmas."

The next morning Mike pulled into Aidan's driveway with Dylan already in the front seat of the extended cab pickup. Aidan said goodbye to his family and got in the back. They drove down the highway and off onto the little dirt road that led to the valley. Mike turned around and backed up to the opening.

"Ok, I'm going to put a pan of water in back and open it up. If you can get him to come to you, bring him to the trailer and see if he'll go inside. If he won't I can dart him, but I'd rather not do that if I don't have to."

"I think he'll come," Aidan said.

Aidan grabbed a ring of bologna and the two friends walked through the cut and into their valley. They walked to their campsite and looked around.

"Well, no new presents," Aidan said.

"That's good, I wonder where he is?" Dylan said.

I'll walk toward the cliffs, you check up on the other side," Aidan said.

They split up and began walking, calling to the cat as they went. Aidan was just below the cave where Spirit had lived when he was healing from the pig battle when he heard a snuff behind him. He turned and there stood Spirit, his tail whipping back and forth.

"Hey boy," Aidan said, "how you been?"

The cat came forward and rubbed his face against Aidan's legs and began purring. Aidan rubbed his head and face. His eyes filled with tears.

"Man, I'm gonna miss this," he said to himself.

"Hey boy... how about a little bologna?" Aidan said reaching in his pocket and pulling out a bag filled with chunks of bologna. The cat was very interested in the meat and Aidan fed him two chunks and then started down the hill with the cat trailing along wanting more.

"Hey, you found him," Dylan said as they got to the valley floor.

Spirit saw Dylan and ran toward him coming up on his back feet as he got to him and knocking him to the ground. "Hey big boy, glad to see me?"

Dylan rough housed with the cat for a bit and then offered him a chunk of the bologna he was carrying.

"I wonder if he likes us or just likes our bologna," he said laughing.

Mike was smiling as the three of them came through the

opening to the valley.

Aidan walked up into the trailer and the cat followed him right in.

"I think I'll ride back here with him at least for a while," Aidan said.

"That might be a good idea so he doesn't get worked all up."

Mike and Dylan shut up the back of the trailer and just as they finished an old pickup pulled off the road and stopped at the end of the dirt track across the field. Clifford got out and walked across the grass.

"What you guys got in the trailer?" he asked.

"I don't see that that's any of your business Clifford?" Dylan said.

"Well we'll see about that. I happen to know you guys have a killer cat in this valley and I've called the sheriff. He should be here any minute.'

"How is a cat any business of yours?"

"I've been helping Mrs. Summers to get justice for her murdered animals."

"Chickens... you dope, they were chickens," Dylan said.

Just then Deputy Biba pulled his squad off the road behind Clifford's truck. He walked over.

"So are you the gentleman who phoned in the emergency?" he said to Clifford.

"Yes sir. These guys have a cougar on this property and I want it confiscated. It's been killing livestock and I'm representing a lady who wants to file a complaint."

Biba looked at Clifford. "Son, are you a lawyer?"

"No, I'm a high school student."

"Then explain to me how you are representing a lady who wants to file a complaint, and how it is you know so much about this cougar when this land is posted?"

"Well, the lady is my friend's ma, and I mistakenly wandered into this valley some time ago and have reason to believe these guys are harboring a killer."

"Mr. Florian, are you harboring a killer?"

Mike grinned and shook his head.

"Dylan, are you harboring a killer?"

"No sir."

Biba looked at Clifford long and hard. "Here's how I see it. You used the 911 system for a non-emergency, which is against the law. You are representing yourself as a lawyer, another crime. And you admitted to trespassing, a third crime."

"But, but they got the cat... it's probably in that trailer right now."

"Here's my advice to you Clifford. Get in your pickup and go home. Find something worthwhile to keep yourself busy and leave these folks alone. If you persist in accusing them I'll have no choice but to take you to jail and if you think those three charges I just mentioned are all I can come up with, just wait until I think a little while about it."

Clifford was speechless.

Mike motioned to Deputy Biba and they stepped in front of Mike's truck.

"You wait Mahoney, you haven't heard the end of this," Clifford said.

Dylan smiled and took the two steps toward Clifford. He cocked back his right fist on the first step and let it go as his second step touched the ground. All of his weight and as much muscle as he could put into the punch slammed into Clifford's right cheek just above the cheekbone. The sound of the fist was like the smack of a ball off a bat.

Clifford stood there for about half a second. His eyes blinked three times and he fell over on his back, out like a light.

Deputy Biba stepped from in front of Mike's truck.

"Did he faint?"

Dylan was massaging his hand. "Yeah, it must be all the excitement."

 Chapter 48

The sound of Aidan laughing came from the trailer and Dylan walked over and looked in one of the fresh air openings they'd left in the sides.

"Jeez, Dyl, what a punch!"

"Did you see that?" Dylan said grinning. "I've been saving that for him for a long time."

"I couldn't hear what was being said, is Deputy Biba on board with what we're doing?"

"Yeah Mike explained it to him and he's all for it."

"Sounds good. Hey can you get one of those camp chairs from Mike's truck for me? I think I'll ride back here with Spirit so he feels less lonely. If I need anything I'll call you on my cell phone."

Dylan went to the truck and got one of the chairs and also grabbed a rolled up sleeping bag. He opened the back of the truck and Spirit came to the doorway, his tail swishing back and forth.

"Going on a big trip Spirit," Dylan said rubbing his face. "You and Aidan behave back here."

Aidan smiled. "We'll be fine. Let's get going before anything else happens. I hated to see Clifford but I'd really hate to see Sonny's mom coming."

Dylan locked up the back of the trailer and got in with Mike into the cab of the truck.

"Aidan's riding back there."

Mike nodded. "Well, we're off then," he said.

It was a little rough riding in the trailer for the first miles but once they got on the highway and then the interstate it smoothed out and Aidan and the cat both napped. Aidan's phone rang about four hours later.

"There's a wildlife area coming up. Mike thought we should

stop for a pit stop. It's pretty secluded so Spirit will be able to get out and stretch his legs. There's a rope with a loop on the end coiled up on a spike on the wall in there. See if he'll let you put it around his neck, just so we can keep him from wandering off."

"Good idea... we're ready any time."

A few minutes later they pulled into a wildlife area that had nature trails and hunting areas. Dylan let Aidan and the cat out and they walked around the area stopping now and then for Spirit to spread his scent on the bushes. They ate a couple of sandwiches and fed Spirit a ring of bologna and then loaded back up and headed west.

The next time they stopped they were just a few miles from the Minnesota/South Dakota border at a remote campground. They drove through the place and only saw one other campsite being used so they went as far from that one as possible and set up their tent and built a fire.

"We made pretty good time today," Mike said. "We'll cross into South Dakota tomorrow morning and then go on to Wyoming. I think we can make it by evening. I'll call my friend and tell him to expect us in the late afternoon."

"That soon huh?" Aidan said.

"Yeah, I know you're not in a big hurry but the sooner we get there, the better it'll be for the cat. It's time for him to be in a place where he's safe and has a chance of finding a mate."

Aidan nodded. "I know, but I still hate to see it happen. We're a part of something so special that I just know it'll never happen again and it's hard to lose it."

Mike and Dylan slept in the tent and Aidan and the cat slept in the trailer. Aidan spread his sleeping bag out on the floor and laid down in it. The cat stood there looking at him for a while and then curled up next to his feet and went to sleep.

The next morning they set out again going north and then west. They made a couple of pit stops on the way and crossed into Wyoming in the afternoon. Mike knew where he was going and a couple of hours later they turned onto a dirt road that led out across the prairie. As they came up over a knoll Dylan saw the farmhouse, barn and other buildings of the ranch.

"Wow, this is really out in the middle of nowhere," he said.

"My friend has twenty thousand acres. It's a huge ranch. He's a good guy. He'll see to it that Spirit has a good long life."

As they pulled into the yard a man came out of the house. He was probably in his mid-fifties, tan and lean. He had a wide smile as he and Mike hugged.

"Dang long time since I've seen you Mikey. How've you been?"

"I'm doing great John. I'm working on another book and keeping busy. This cougar has kind of gotten me off track but it's been worth it."

"So you say this guy is people friendly?"

Mike nodded to Dylan. He went over and opened the back of the trailer and Aidan came out leading the cat by the rope. They walked over to the man and Mike.

"John, this is Aidan, and his friend there is Dylan, and this furry one is Spirit."

The man stood there staring at the cougar. "He let's you lead him? I'd of never thought that was possible."

Aidan nodded. "He eats out of our hand, and he likes to have his face rubbed. He's kind of like a barn cat but on a much larger scale."

John just shook his head. "Unbelievable."

Chapter 49

"Well we better get him to his new home," Mike said.

Aidan and Dylan looked at him and nodded. "Yeah, I guess so," Aidan said quietly.

"I've been seeing "Little Girl" a lot lately in the north range. She's the younger female in the area. Her range overlaps where the male used to live and he mated with her a couple of years ago. She raised two kittens but they're gone off somewhere on their own. "Big Girl", the older female is south of here. I haven't seen her for a month but I'm sure she's still out there. I think he'd like "Little Girl", and she'd like him, she's probably ready to raise another litter."

Dylan grinned. "Hear that Spirit? You might get lucky."

They all laughed and then they decided to follow John out onto the prairie where he thought the female would be. John drove ahead of them in his jeep. They drove for a long way, maybe six miles and John stopped on a little rise and got out. They parked the truck and walked up to John.

"This is her range," he said.

They got Spirit out of the trailer and Aidan took the rope off his neck. His stomach felt like it had a rock in it. He felt his eyes filling.

Dylan knelt down and hugged the cat. "You have a good life buddy. I've sure had a good time knowing you." He turned to Aidan with tears in his eyes and smiled sadly. Then he walked back to the truck.

Mike smiled and patted Aidan on the back. "Take your time," he said.

"I'm going to walk him a little way," Aidan said.

The rest of them stood and watched as he and the cat walked down the rise. Spirit walked right at Aidan's side, leaning into him. He put his hand on the cat's head and petted him as they walked.

When they got to the next rise Aidan stopped and knelt down in front of the cat. His eyes were filled with tears and he had a huge lump in his throat. He put his hands on either side of the cat's face and rubbed him.

"This is as far as I go boy. This is your new home. You'll be safe here and can find a girlfriend and it'll be real good for you."

Spirit looked deep into Aidan's eyes and leaned forward and nuzzled him.

Aidan's heart was breaking. He hugged the cat and then stood up.

"Now go."

He motioned with his arm toward the prairie.

The cat walked a little way away and looked back.

"Go on," Aidan said.

Spirit loped across the flat and stopped short of the next rise. He sniffed the air and sprinted up the hill and disappeared over the top.

Tears were running down Aidan's face as he watched him

182

go. He finally turned and started walking back toward the others. When he was just about to the top of the hill where the others were Dylan pointed.

"Aidan look!"

Aidan turned and looked. Spirit and another cougar, smaller and daintier stood on the next rise. Spirit's tail was whipping back and forth. The two cats stood there for several minutes and then the female rubbed up against Spirit and she turned to go down the back side of the hill. Spirit watched her go and turned back toward the boys. He looked at the female and then back at the boys. Then he turned toward the female. He stopped just before he went over the side and looked back at them for a long minute, and then he disappeared.

About the Author

Dan Bomkamp has made his home in the Wisconsin River valley all his life with the exception of his college years in La Crosse. He has been an avid hunter and fisherman his whole life. For many years he was in the sporting goods industry and began writing in the 80s for outdoor magazines. He is active in the Foreign Exchange Student program having hosted 33 boys from 13 countries over the years. Golden Retrievers have also been a big part of his life. He had at least one Golden sharing his home for 33 years. He lives in Muscoda with his cat Tigger and his Boston Terrier Buster.

His previous books are: *The Adventures of Thunderfoot; More Adventures of Thunderfoot; Thanks Thunderfoot; The Best of Thunderfoot; The Gosey; Big Edna—Back to the Gosey; Voyageur; Lost Flight; Tag; Whiteout.*

Check out his website: www.danbomkamp.com
Or you can email him: danbomkamp@live.com